FAITHLESS

BOOK 1
OF

A VISION OF VAMPIRES

By Laura Legend

court

Tom

I am

King County

408-536-6000

addse

150.00
60.00
210.00

$3680-

2nd

First edition

EPub Edition August 2018
Print Edition September 2018

ISBN: 9781723791192

Printed in the United Sates of America

For Buffy and Faith, my favorite badass vampire slayers

Prologue

FATHER MARQUAND SAT up with a jerk from his unintended nap, dropping his half-read copy of *Codependent No More* onto the floor, wiping the drool from his chin.

What the hell? he thought with a flash of anger—and then immediately felt bad for cursing.

Someone was pounding on his thick wooden door. The whole cottage seemed to shake. Three thundering knocks—thump, thump, thump. The knocks were heavy but slow. Whoever was at the door, he was careful to keep those beats evenly spaced. Father Marquand pictured an ogre of a mathematician knocking on his door, someone strong enough to rattle the glass in his windows but with the suspenders, white socks, and pocket protector to account for the care and precision.

The knocks came again, but faster now.

The sound was commanding.

The sun was setting. Dark clouds were moving in. The wind was picking up, cold and sharp as the night approached.

The priest sighed. *I'm coming, I'm coming! Hold your horses.*

His bones ached at the sudden cold front rushing in. He would never make it to the chapel in time for evening prayers, now. He hurried to the door and then, when he got there, hesitated at the thought of opening it. He couldn't quite the shake the image of an enormous and angry accountant waiting for him on the other side of the door.

While he dithered, an orange tabby cat curled between his legs and almost tripped him. He started to curse the cat and then stopped short, trying to remember if he even owned a cat.

Get a hold of yourself, old man. Get to the door! What if it's Christ himself, or one of his apostles, finally come to see you? Have some faith!

With a trembling hand, Father Marquand pulled the door open and stepped out of the way. A thin, slight man in a dark, sharply cut suit stood on his welcome mat. Backlit in the doorway by the sun's fading light, his eyes were deep in shadow, but his teeth flashed white.

This man was decidedly not Jesus.

"I have come at the agreed upon time," the thin man said calmly as he smoothed a lock of dark hair back into place. "May I enter?" The man's voice was formal, his tone measured. The accent was flat and homeless, unplaceable.

The priest did not respond. He stared back at the man, confused, his mouth hanging open. How could this slight man make his whole house shake? How could he command him with a knock? And where was his protractor?

"We have an appointment," the thin man continued. "I am here about the holy relic that recently came into your possession. I must see it. Please bring it to me immediately."

"What? Who? Who are you again?" Father Marquand managed to say, wringing his hands.

"You *must* remember our appointment," the man cut in. "Perhaps you are tired, and have simply forgotten?"

Father Marquand did feel disoriented. And deeply tired. His limbs ached with exhaustion. "I ... yes, I am quite tired." How had he forgotten how tired he was?

"So," the stranger continued, his voice hardening, "the relic?"

Like a puppet on strings, the priest found himself turning to retrieve the relic. But before he could get very far, the man interrupted him.

"But first," the thin man said, "you must invite me in."

"Yes, certainly," he responded hurriedly. He could feel the need to fulfill this man's requests growing in his mind, spreading like ink in water, blotting out every other thought. "Please, please, sir, come right in."

The gaunt man frowned, paused for a moment at the door's threshold, and then stepped decisively into the room. The walls of the house seemed to bow slightly outward and the house lights momentarily dimmed and flickered. But everything returned to normal so quickly the priest couldn't tell if that impression was real or just imagined. He shook off the feeling of panic that gripped his old heart. The cat hissed and bolted out the door.

Calm down. You're so tired that you're acting crazy. And quick, bring him what he came for!

While the priest fetched the relic, the thin man took stock of the priest's bare, shabby room. He ran a gloved finger across the window sill, leaving a trail in the dust. He frowned again and brushed off his hands.

"Here you are, here you are, sir," the priest said, rushing back into the room, his hands clutched protectively around a small package. "Here is the relic. See for yourself."

Father Marquand held out the relic, cradled in his hands, wrapped in a thick, brown cloth. The priest folded back its layers to reveal the object hidden inside: a very plain and very old piece of wood.

The thin man flinched when he saw it, but, drawing a deep breath, steeled himself to lean in for a closer look. Beautiful. And dangerous. He was mesmerized by the sight of it.

He took a step closer and pulled the leather glove off his right hand. Most of the flesh of this hand was black and necrotic. Father Marquand stared.

Time seemed to slow. The wind stopped howling, the clouds stopped moving, and everything went quiet. The house itself seemed to hold its breath.

The man reached out with his rotting hand. The relic began to tremble and glow and the flesh of the thin man's hand, haloed by this glow, appeared to heal.

But just as the thin man was about to touch the wood itself, the priest suddenly shook himself awake, as if he'd still been dreaming up until that moment, and jerked the relic out of reach. He quickly wrapped it up again, pulling it protectively against his chest.

In response, the thin man straightened his tie, adjusted the cuff of his jacket, and slipped his glove back on.

"How much?" he asked. "What is your price?"

"I, I—" the priest stuttered. No matter how tired he was, there was no way he would willingly sell this relic—if it is what he thought it was, he'd been looking for it his whole life!—and especially not to this strange, thin man whose hooded eyes cut into his soul.

He gathered his courage: "This relic is not for sale, sir. And certainly it's not for sale to you."

"How much?" the thin man hissed.

The priest remained silent.

"Do not make me ask again," the stranger said, almost whispering now.

"I, I said—"

"*How much*," the thin man asked a third time, stepping in close to the priest. "Three is a powerful number, as you well know Father. I have asked three times and I *will* have what I came for."

"We're done here," the priest gulped, retreating down the hall. "Please leave … now …"

"Oh, Father, it's too late for that now. You already invited me in." The thin man sighed with regret. Curious. The priest had been fairly certain those hard eyes were incapable of regret.

The stranger adjusted both of his black gloves, flexing his hands. He met the priest's eyes, rooting him to the spot. He stepped close and gently whispered in the priest's ear.

"Oh, Father. Dear Father. It's too late for you. And I will have what I came for."

* * *

The sun had long since set by the time the thin man returned home. His rooms were dark and dry and cold. The furnishings were expensive but spare.

He carefully removed his gloves and hung his tailored jacket on a wooden hanger. He washed his hands methodically, like a surgeon, up to his elbows, careful to remove any lingering dirt or blood. He examined his right hand in the bright bathroom light, noting how the blackness was starting to creep beyond his hand and up his arm, following the lines of his veins.

He may have less time left than he'd thought. He needed to finish his work.

He dried his hand and buttoned his shirt sleeves. He sat down at his desk, the relic centered on his blotter. He considered it for a moment and then, leaving its wrapping intact, hefted its unnaturally heavy weight in his hand.

"You," he whispered to the relic, "are precious to me. And soon, everything will be ready."

He unlocked a display case and added the piece to his collection.

"Soon."

1

FOR A TWENTY-six-year-old barista, Cassandra Jones had some unusual skills. Forget her grad work in archeology —what barista worth their salt wasn't a failed PhD?—or even the swords in the trunk of her car. No, what really made Cass unusual was that she saw right through people. She could tell right away when people were lying. She could tell, in her bones, if something was true.

For Cass, figuring out the truth was the easy part. The hard part was figuring out *why*.

She could tell if someone was a liar, but that didn't mean she could understand why people did what they did. Sometimes she felt like she could almost hear her cat thinking out loud—"Scratch behind my ears! Bring me some Fancy Feast! Find me a giant cat-pyramid filled with cat-sized tunnels! Never buy a dog!" But *people*, on the other hand, were all black boxes. She didn't understand them. And, often enough, this made it hard to like them.

She could tell, for instance, that she was probably *not* going to understand this lady that had just walked into the coffeehouse. And she was sure she wasn't going to like her.

The lady walked into Java's Palace like she owned the place. She didn't look like a Hutt, but she sure acted like one. She was in her late forties, platinum blond, big diamond ring, boob job, chin tuck, expensive yoga clothes, botox around the eyes, laughing too loudly on her phone.

The lady saw Cass from across the room and, first thing, her voice dropped and her eyes narrowed. She didn't like what she saw as she sized Cass up.

Cass was beautiful in a careless way. She didn't style her dark hair, she just pulled it into a sloppy ponytail. She didn't worry about clothes, she just slipped into a t-shirt and an old pair of jeans. She didn't wear make-up, she just washed her face in the morning. She wasn't tall, but she didn't need to be.

Cass tried to ignore the lady. She looked back at her phone. Between customers she'd been trying to secure her entry into an underground mixed martial arts tournament. Her thumbs flew. She had to get this squared away before the deadline tonight.

Out of the corner of her eye, she saw Zach, her friend and fellow barista, watching her as he put the finishing touches on another latte. From the crooked smile on his face, she could tell he was already anxious to see what would happen when this diva finally made her way to the counter.

The lady jammed her huge, pink, bedazzled phone into her purse and strutted up to the register, wobbling in her absurd heels as they click-clacked on the polished concrete floor.

Cass started taking bets in her own head—offering generous three-to-one odds to all imaginary takers—that the lady would tip over before she made it to the counter.

Also, who wears heels with yoga pants? Cass barely avoided saying out loud.

She was almost done with her text. The lady arrived with a minor crash, flopping her purse next to the register and trying to look casual as she leaned against the counter for support.

Without looking, Cass held up a finger to ask the lady to wait just a moment longer.

This lady was not going to wait. She cleared her throat and launched into a complicated order, not caring if Cass was ready.

"Hey, I want a caramel macchiato, venti, skim—no, soy—extra shot and extra hot with extra whip, sugar free and caffeine free. To go. And hurry, I've got a pedicure in ten!"

So, you want a coffee, but without any caffeine, sugar, fat, or taste. Got it. One Crazy Bitch Coffee coming up. In just … one … second …

Case still didn't look at her. She finished the last line of the text, hit send, and sighed with relief to have that off her plate.

She turned to the woman, looked up, and, for the first time, their eyes met. Or, their eyes *almost* met.

This was the part Cass hated. This was part where she never quite connected with other people.

Cass had a lazy eye. She'd had it since birth. The muscles needed to focus that eye had never fully developed. The result was that, from across the room, Cass was a knock-out. But once people got up close and tried to make eye contact, they didn't know which eye to look at and generally just got confused and annoyed. Cass's eyes were dark, the lashes long, and their slight tilt hinted at the fact that, on her father's side, she was fourth generation Japanese-American. But there was no helping it: the wobbly-eye-thing just freaked people out.

The lady visibly recoiled.

Geez. It's not like I'm trying to freak you out. Cass looked down and pretended to prep her register in a helpful way.

Recovering from the initial shock, the lady now looked like she might laugh, but she managed to rein herself in with just a huge, snarky smile.

Cass tried to get things back on track.

"Ma'am?" Cass asked. "Ma'am? Could you please repeat your order?"

The lady didn't respond. She just looked around the room as if to say, *Have you guys seen this?*

Cass had had enough. *What do people want from me anyway? What do they expect? Nobody's perfect.* She could feel the hot hand of frustration on the back of her neck.

"Ma'am, give me your order or get out of line. People are waiting," Cass snapped.

"How *dare* you," the lady snarled in return, back in her element. "You ignore me and then insult me? I won't stand for it. I'm important. I've got places to go. My driver, Mr. Andropov, is waiting for me. I don't have time for your nonsense and backtalk. I want to speak to the manager. Immediately."

Cass groaned inside. She already regretted her frustration. This piece of work wasn't worth it.

"Immediately!" the lady almost shrieked.

Cass looked over at Zach as she went to get the manager but he just frowned and shrugged his shoulders. There was nothing to be done now.

Her manager was not pleased. She'd already heard the ruckus through her door. She was trying to catch up with last week's episodes of *The Young and the Restless*. She stood up slowly and shook her head in a theatrically disappointed way.

"Cass, go on break. *Now*."

The manager said it loud enough that everyone in the coffeehouse could hear. This was a performance for the sake of the lady. But, still, Cass didn't like the tone of her manager's voice. She'd been fired before and she knew what that tone sounded like. She didn't need any kind of truth-powers to tell she really was in trouble here.

The manager arrived at the counter with a flourish, like she was a knight come to rescue this trophy wife in distress. The lady started to rattle off a long list of complaints about Cass, most of them manufactured on the spot. She clearly had a deep reservoir of experience to draw on when it came to professional-grade retail complaining. The manager listened patiently and nodded along the whole time.

"I'm so sorry ma'am, I'll take care of everything. Now, what would you like? It's on us, of course! And here's a gift card for next time ..."

Cass couldn't quite hear the woman's reply, but she recognized that tone. *Snippy, entitled ...* She shook her head. *So* not worth it right now.

"Yes, I agree ..." The manager's voice floated back towards the break room. "Oh, wow! I *love* that bedazzled phone case you have there ... great taste, so you!"

Cass was done. She grabbed her jacket and stepped out into the alley. The moon was rising. She pinched the front of her jacket closed against the cold evening wind and took a deep breath. An orange tabby cat slipped out from behind the dumpster and out the far end of the alley.

Wait, was that my cat? she wondered. This seemed unlikely; her apartment was miles from here.

But before she could call after the cat to see what would happen, her phone buzzed.

It was a text from a number she didn't recognize, just eight precise words that froze her in place.

I have read your dissertation. We need to talk.

2

"WHAT. THE HELL. Is this?" Cass wondered aloud.

The wind was blowing harder now and loose garbage fluttered around the alley. An obnoxious fluorescent light above the service door hummed and buzzed.

There couldn't be more than a handful of people in the world that even knew she'd written a dissertation. The work was unfinished and unpublished. That little hitch in her path to academic stardom was why she was working as a barista in the first place. Her cheeks burned red just thinking about it. If this coffeeshop alleyway wasn't a million miles from where she'd hoped to be, it was close.

Who is this? she texted back. *How did you get this number?*

She stared at the screen, willing a response. She paced the alley and kicked at some of the garbage on the ground, warming her free hand under her opposite arm, her eyes still glued to the phone.

The appearance of a speech bubble with three dots indicated that the mystery person was typing a response. She waited, impatient.

A second message appeared: *Who I am is immaterial. Your work is all that matters.*

Was this Zach pulling a prank on her? Was this her Dad trying to make her feel better about bombing out of her doctoral program? In her mind, she spooled through the faces of friends and acquaintances, looking for a possible match. Nobody fit the bill.

Who on earth could this be?

She almost dropped her phone when it buzzed again and a third message appeared: *We MUST locate all of the pieces of the One True Cross. Your work on this topic is the key. It is too important to sit in a drawer. It could open doors that have been locked for thousands of years. And time is growing short. Please meet with me.*

Cass felt her weak eye twitch and almost swim into focus in response, registering the truth of this statement like a lie detector. But she didn't like the feel of this conversation. Just because this was the truth didn't mean it was something good.

Her free hand felt for the pendant she always wore around her neck. It used to be her mother's. She rubbed it absently between her thumb and index finger.

Her work on how to locate the missing pieces of the One True Cross *was* original and groundbreaking. She didn't disagree about that. And she wasn't just being vain. Her committee didn't reject her research because the work was shoddy. They rejected it because they were afraid of what it would mean if she was right.

But, still, that didn't mean she was going to start spending her free time texting with anonymous wackos about her scholarship. That was a shortcut to crazy town, and she didn't live that far away as it was.

She made a firm decision.

You've got the wrong number, she texted back. *Get lost.*

She slipped her phone into her back pocket and leaned against the wall. She looked up into the sky.

Just as she started to relax again, Zach banged through the coffeehouse service door, backing into the alley, hauling a bunch of trash bags.

Cass jumped.

"Jesus, Zach!" Cass said.

Zach tossed the garbage bags into the dumpster, then stretched his arms high above his head, flexing his triceps. He held the pose for a long, comic moment before dropping his arms to his sides and brushing his hands together to signal a job well done. He turned to face her and caught her admiring him.

"Take a good look," he said, teasing her. "Looks are free. But more than that is going to cost you. And I'm not sure you can afford it."

He finished with a wink and a crooked smile.

Cass laughed him off, grateful for a bright note in a hard day. She owed Zach this job in the first place. They had originally met at an underground MMA tournament. She was fighting. He was working the room with drinks as a waiter.

Zachary Riviera wasn't really her type—she tended toward the serious and brooding—but he was about her age, pleasantly fit, his dark mop of hair and Latin complexion were cute, and he *loved* history. This last part, above all, had sold her. He was a voracious reader, but self-taught. He was full of questions once he found out about her work and they became fast friends. He didn't mind her lazy eye. He found it endearing, a chink in her otherwise perfect armor.

When he learned that she was trapped in career limbo, he offered to help her find some work while she decided what to do with her life. And now here they were, alone in a dark alley behind a coffeeshop.

Success?

"Kill me now," she responded, leaning back against the alley wall again, back of her hand to her forehead, pretending to faint.

"I don't think I'll have to. It looks like either the customers or the manager are going to get there first."

She stuck out her tongue at him and then frowned at the conversation's serious turn.

"Listen, Cass." Zach said, a dark note creeping into his voice. "If you get fired, how are you going to make your rent? And who's going to keep me company here? Who's going to fill me in about the location of the holy grail? And, most importantly, who's going to clean those disgusting bathrooms every hour, on the hour, if you're not here? Not me. If you get fired, I'll have to quit too. We'll both get thrown out on the street, you'll have to sell all those way-too-realistic swords you own just to have money for food, and eventually we'll both end up living under benches in the park, stealing bread crumbs from local pigeons."

He paused for dramatic effect.

"It just seems like a slippery slope, you know? Totally not worth it."

He almost made it to the end of his monologue without cracking a smile, but his eyes were shining the whole way through and his final words trailed into a laugh.

"You moron," Cass answered. "Grow up."

She gave him a friendly shove and he pretended to stumble back against the alley wall. She pounded one fist into her other open hand, like she was coming for him.

"I see how it is," Zach said. "I knew this moment was coming any day now. You think that because you know jujitsu and shit that you can just have your way with me. Well, it doesn't work like that. Even if I let you have my body, I'll never give up my soul." He pressed his back flat against the brick wall, cringing, closed his eyes with his head turned to the side, and then puckered up like he was in a kid's cartoon.

She almost laughed but stopped herself. She was half-tempted to call his bluff and kiss him just to teach him a lesson. That *would* shut him up.

She stepped in close and let him feel her breath on his neck. He squirmed and then peeked out through a half-open eye to see what she was doing.

She grabbed him by his stubbly chin and turned his face toward her.

"You're going to get it now—" she started.

But then the alley door banged open and the manager yelled for them.

They were out of time.

Was she relieved or disappointed?

"Zach, back to the front," the manager barked.

"And Jones, we need to talk. In my office. Now."

3

Cass knew she was in trouble when the manager asked her to "please, take a seat" in her office.

The office was cramped and overflowing with old sales reports and used order forms. Boxes of leftover holiday coffee cups lined one wall.

Is it possible to be crushed to death under an avalanche of unused holiday cups decorated with non-denominational snowflakes and bells? Cass wondered. *And if so, would that really be so sad?*

If this meeting dragged on too long, maybe death-by-styrofoam-cup was the kind of noble death she'd be willing to settle for.

Cass tried to manufacture some humility. She kept her eyes down and worked to look penitent. Plus, maybe this way she could keep her lazy eye out of the conversation.

Her manager settled into her chair with a groan. She had positioned herself strategically behind her desk, like its laminated wood was her first line of defense against bad employees.

"You know you can't treat customers like that," her manager began.

"But …" Cass began.

"No buts. You know the corporate spiel. The customer is always right. We're here to serve, blah, blah, blah. It may be a load of crap, but it's the load of crap we live by."

I deserve this, Cass told herself. *I messed up. I just need to take my medicine here and move on. It is my own stupid fault that this crazy, bedazzled, high-heeled, yoga-pants-wearing trophy wife …*

Spying the look of frustration creeping into Cass's face, the manager sighed and leaned forward in her chair.

Whoops, Cass thought, *lost my own thread there. Try again. Right. I deserve this. Keep my head down. Move on. Look contrite.*

"Look. We don't all have fancy graduate degrees or parents that run big university libraries. Some of us are just simple, working class folk and we have to squeeze a living out of whatever kind of work we can find."

Cass bobbed her head, nodding agreement, but didn't look up.

The manager paused and tried a different tack.

"Knowing so much about history like you do, think about it like this."

She grabbed two used styrofoam cups, an unopened box, and couple of twisty-tied sleeves of cups from the shelf and set them on her desk.

"Java's Palace is your feudal lord," she continued. "And you are its loyal indentured servant. You are a serf working for the glory of your lord."

She slid the box to the center of her desk and stacked sleeves of cups at the box's four corners like towers for a castle.

She held up one stained cup and put it on top of the box. "This is your feudal lord, Java Palace."

She held up the other used cup, crumpled it a little, and then set it next to the box, somewhere near Thanksgiving on her out-of-date desk calendar. "This is you, loyal serf, muddy and covered in filth, down in the field, slaving away for coffee beans."

She gestured broadly, pleased with her tableau.

"Maybe, once upon a time, you used to live in the castle with the other fancy cups—I mean, fancy people—but now you're down in the mud with the rest of us. And, being down in the mud with the rest of us, this means that when any nipped-and-tucked trophy wife pops in for her $15 latte and asks you to jump, the only response you ever give is to ask how high."

She crossed her arms and leaned back in her squeaky chair.

Cass nodded her head again, hoping that her sorry face was convincing, but worried about the objection bubbling up inside of her.

"And under no circumstances—no, be quiet, I'm talking now—and under no circumstance are you to ever give any of these paying, respectable, hard-working customers the *evil eye*. Do you understand me?"

Cass swallowed hard and tried to nod.

"No. Evil. Eye."

That last bit seemed unnecessary.

"Yes, ma'am," she said.

Cass could feel a flicker of frustration starting to grow. She rubbed her mother's pendant between her fingers. It felt hot in her hand.

"Also," the manager continued, "there is a strict company policy against using your phone while working the counter. If I see you pulling that stunt again, you'll be done here. I won't tolerate it."

That, Cass could tell, was true. Her manager was serious. If she got caught, she'd be done. She didn't know if she could take being fired again.

"I don't need the trouble," the manager said. "And don't think Zach can save you. The dimples in his cheeks are cute but they aren't magic. I'll fire both your asses. I've got a whole stack of applications from unemployed grad students like you and every one of them would be grateful to have your job. I could fire you now and have your position filled by someone with graduate training in Renaissance poetry before we closed tonight."

This last bit made Cass's eye twitch. It was true that the manager wouldn't hesitate to fire Cass but she was lying about how easy it would be to replace her. She

didn't want the trouble of finding and training some-
body new. And, despite her poor people skills, Cass was
dependable.

It's okay, she thought. *You can do this. She needs you.
Just try to see things from her perspective.*

Still trying to keep her head down, Cass glanced up
at her boss, trying to take her in.

*What was her perspective? Who was this lady? What
was she really like? What did she want? Who did she love?
What did she think about when she didn't have to think
about anything else?*

Cass had no idea. This woman, like most everyone,
was a puzzle box, locked up tight. It was like Cass's
power to see the truth and look right *through* people
made it harder for her to actually look *at* them and
understand them.

All of this was rooted, for Cass, in the fact that her
own emotions felt distant and foreign. Her own emotions always seemed one step removed, as if she were
watching herself in a movie, as if they didn't quite be-
long to her. She could sense her emotions banging
around inside of her, locked up behind a heavy door,
but she couldn't quite *feel* the emotions themselves, first
hand. And, unable to grasp her own emotions and
motivations in the first person, she often found herself
at a loss to understand anyone else's feelings either.

As she remembered it, this problem had gotten
much worse after her mother's death, but there had
always been signs that something wasn't right with her
emotions. In elementary school, her teachers had picked

up on this right away. They'd sent Cass to be poked and tested. And then the doctors had started throwing around words like "antisocial personality disorder" and recommended that they start experimenting with different kinds of medication for Cass.

But Cass's mom wouldn't hear any of it. She was ferocious. "She's a *kid*, not a *problem*," she'd spit back at them.

So what if Cass was different? This didn't mean that the school or the doctors needed to medicate that difference right of her. Cass didn't need to be to squeezed into a more normal shape just so she would be easier for *other* people to handle.

"Different doesn't mean broken," her mom would say again and again like a mantra.

One day, after the last of these appointments, her mom had taken her to the park. It was a warm day, early in the fall. The trees were just starting to change and the afternoon sun was high and bright. They bought some ice cream from a cart and sat on a low, wooden bench. Cass loved ice cream and she worked hard to keep it from dripping down the side of her cone.

When she was done with her cone, her mother turned serious. She took Cass's hand in hers and looked her in both eyes.

"Don't worry, Cass," she said. "We'll work it out ourselves. There's nothing wrong with you. We don't need these doctors or their theories or their medications. You and me, we have each other."

Cass could remember this moment with perfect clarity. This memory never aged. She could see the sunlight. She could hear the timbre of her mom's voice. She could feel the strength in her mom's hands.

And what her mother said was true. They did have each other. Her mom protected her and stood up for her. Her mom was the only one who seemed to understand her.

But then, when she was eleven, her mom died. And her dad did what he could, but her dad was not her mom. And now here she was, twenty-six years old, and her mom was long gone and there was no one to help her and she *still* didn't understand other people.

"Jones?" her manager interrupted. "Are you hearing me, Jones?"

Cass squeezed her pendant and came back to the present.

"Yes, ma'am," Cass said.

Her manager flattened the stained cup that had been the feudal serf and tossed it into the garbage can.

"One more time and you're done here."

"Yes, ma'am."

"Clock out and go home. You're done for the day."

4

THE THIN MAN was in a hotel in Paris. Though the sun had barely set in Salem, Oregon for Cassandra Jones, it was closer to sunrise here.

From a penthouse on the top floor, he looked out over the city. Two of the outer walls of his penthouse were made entirely of glass and they offered a breathtaking panorama of the city of lights. Though he had tired of many things over the course of his very long life, he had never tired of this view. He came back to this hotel—and to this room in particular—again and again, whenever his work permitted.

Except for a single desk lamp, the room's lights were off. The room's temperature was set low. He liked it cold. And, too, he liked how the single light from his desk caused part of his room to be reflected in the enormous window, superimposing a partial image of the room onto the glowing Parisian skyline. The desk, the lamp, his open laptop—everything that fell within the arc of the lamp's light was reflected in the glass.

Everything, that is, but him. His own pale, thin frame was invisible in the glass.

This made him feel both powerful and alone.

He reached out and tapped the glass—one, two, three—softly, the beats evenly spaced. He always felt restless at this time of night.

He held up his gloved right hand, catching the light from his desk. He flexed the hand and then winced. He flexed it again and again until he had mastered the pain and his hand was steady. He considered removing his black glove but decided against it.

What would be the difference between looking at this lifeless black glove and his dying black hand? he wondered.

The thin man turned his attention back to the window, his reflection still absent. He hadn't seen his own likeness in what seemed like forever. He had forgotten, really, what his own face looked like.

Though it was four in the morning, he was still fully and impeccably dressed. He brushed some imaginary lint from the shoulder of his tailored jacket and straightened his already straight tie clip. In the modern age of mirrors, his concern for his appearance had grown increasingly neurotic. He was always checking with his hands to make sure everything was in place. This kind of obsessive compulsion was, perhaps, an inevitable side-effect of not having a reflection. He couldn't stop checking for what he could no longer see.

This particular tick was relatively new for the thin man. But it had always been true that he could not trust what he could not see. He'd never been big on blind faith. He needed evidence. He only trusted things that were concrete and countable.

That was why he had never been able to bring himself to trust the Nazarene—everything the man said seemed so intangible and counter-intuitive. But the cross the Romans had hung him from, that was a different story. The pieces of the One True Cross were something that could be collected and counted and held. He could feel in his unnatural bones the power of the fragments he'd already managed to collect. He could feel their power to heal him and, more, elevate him. Only a handful of pieces still escaped him.

This was why he needed Cassandra Jones's help.

He hadn't expected her to respond positively to his anonymous texts—though it might have been convenient if she had. He was just trying to stir the pot. He was setting her in motion so that she would be of use to him whether she wanted to be or not.

Even now, several other pieces of his plan were already in motion. A handful of his colleagues would soon pay her a visit to make sure she wasn't tempted to slip back into the numb routine of her normal life.

Though, truth be told, there was nothing normal or ordinary about Cassandra Jones. Whatever it cost her, he would at least make sure her life was never ordinary again.

The thin man sat down at the room's desk, sleepless. He scrolled through the list of sites, blogs, and discussion boards he used to keep track of any news that might aid his search for the remaining relics. This, for instance, was how he had learned about the holy relic that had recently—and only momentarily—passed through Father Marquand's hands.

Backlists and reddits dedicated to discussing archeology and Christian relics were sometimes useful but generally wacky places. He used a bunch of different names and handles on these lists, sometimes using several different names in the same discussion.

When the lists weren't giving him any useful information, though, he took a kind of wry pleasure in trolling the true-believers who also followed this kind of news. He was excellent at manipulation and he'd had thousands of years to hone his arguments against God's existence, Christ's divinity, and the virgin birth. It wasn't really fair how easily he could dismantle their arguments and send Christian after Christian retreating from the light of reason back into the superstitious darkness of a weak faith.

Still, when it came to these kinds of arguments, he was like a dog with an old bone: there wasn't any meat left to eat on these bones but he couldn't quite stop himself from gnawing at them anyway. No matter how tight his proofs, something always seemed unfinished about them.

When he'd made his rounds on the blogs and backlists, he switched to Twitter. He was just sinking his teeth into a new conversation with a desk clerk from the Creation Museum in Petersburg, KY, when his phone buzzed.

"Yes," he said simply. Small talk was beyond him.

He listened silently for several minutes, patiently gathering the facts without interruption.

When his subordinate had finished, he simply and icily said, "Text me details about the location."

He ended the call, stood up, tightened the knot in his tie, and looked out the window facing east. One of the final missing pieces of the Cross may have just been located in Valencia, Spain.

It was time to gather his things.

He had work to do before the sun rose.

5

CASS WAS HOME before nine. She lived alone in an old studio apartment on top of a Thai noodle place not far from the university. After living here for two years, even the thought of green curry turned her stomach— though she figured she'd probably have to live here another thirty years before she'd get sick of the mango sticky rice. The trade-offs were worth it, though. The loft's ceilings were high, its unfinished brick walls were set wide, and there were no neighbors to complain about her playing music too loud, keeping odd hours, or yelling "hi-yah!" at the top of her lungs.

She tossed her keys in a basket on the kitchen counter and doffed her jacket. Her mail was all garbage and went straight into the recycling bin. She put some food in the cat's dish and called for him.

"Atlantis. Here kitty-kitty," she said.

But the cat was nowhere to be found. Even if she locked all the windows and doors, the cat came and went as he pleased. He would disappear for days at a time, lost. That's why Cass had named him Atlantis in the first place.

"Stupid cat. Where are you when I need you?"

She slumped into the soft arms of an overstuffed yellow leather couch that had already been curb-worthy when she'd inherited it forever ago.

I love you, couch, she thought. *You're my longest, most successful relationship. You never judge me or yell at me. You never disappear like my cat. You just let me sink into your old leathery arms and hold me tight. We understand each other.*

She patted the couch arm and affectionately traced a crack in the leather with her finger, then reached between two cushions looking for the remote control. Instead of finding the remote, she pulled out thirty-seven cents and a small, black bra she couldn't swear was actually hers.

What the …? Whose … ? She shuddered and stuffed the money and underwear back into the darkness she'd fished them from. Maybe she and the couch didn't know each other as well as she'd thought.

She was tired but her crazy day had left her wired rather than sleepy. Maybe she could fix that with some exercise.

Tracking down some clean gym clothes seemed like a lot of trouble, so Cass just kicked off her shoes and jeans. She lifted a wooden practice sword off the hook where it hung on the wall and spun the sword through the opening moves of her practice routine. She had studied sword fighting and martial arts for more than a decade, with both Eastern and Western styles and weapons. Over time, she'd fused a bunch of different styles into her own crazy brand of fighting. Opponents had no idea what to do with her in tournaments.

Her goal, now, was to beat the crap out of her Wing Chun practice dummy. At one point, she'd taken a magic marker and drawn a smiley face on the wooden post at the center of its many waving wooden arms. Today, the smile seemed to mock her.

Fine, if that's how you're going to be, she thought, and delivered a handful of blows.

The dummy had seen it all over the years—sometimes playing the part of an almost-boyfriend, sometimes a bedazzled customer, sometimes a coffeehouse manager, sometimes a dissertation director, sometimes her own dad—and had taken everything she could dish out without blinking.

It took her about forty-five minutes to run through the whole routine. By the time she was done she ached with exhaustion and her t-shirt and underwear were soaked through with sweat. She tossed them in the hamper, took a cold shower, pulled on an over-sized shirt she'd slept in for years, and then collapsed on a mattress that, over time, had been crowded into the corner of her apartment by swordplay.

Finally in bed, she flicked on a small fan, wrapped herself in a sheet, closed her eyes, and expected to pass out.

But she still couldn't sleep.

Instead, she found herself thinking about the weird text message she'd gotten in the alley. Apparently her worries about the text had just been waiting for her to relax so they could ambush her. Before she knew it, she was caught in a loop thinking about the text and her dissertation and, in a matter of minutes, she was wide awake again.

"Shit," she groaned out loud.

She rolled out of bed and sorted through the piles of research stacked on her desk until she found what she was looking for: the latest, but still unfinished, draft of her dissertation. She grabbed a spoon and a yogurt from the fridge and sat down at the kitchen table with the manuscript. Sucking on the spoon, she started flipping through its pages.

Though she knew most of the material by heart, she was still fascinated by it. Despite what her dissertation committee had decided, the argument felt right. It felt *true*. The pieces snapped together with a satisfying click and, in the end, they added up to something substantial and surprising: a template, a method, for finding real relics of the One True Cross and sifting them from the fakes.

But as much as she was still gripped by her work, it was painful to revisit. She felt humiliated whenever she thought about washing out of her doctoral program.

And, more, the work's associations made her feel sad and lost. She'd done most of the project's research and writing while staffing the Hatfield Library help desk at Willamette University in Salem. Re-reading her work now, she could almost smell the books that filled the library's stacks. She could almost hear that weird mix of sounds that mark a library—pages turning, pencils scratching, an occasional cough, the scrape of a wooden chair on a marble floor. She missed it. She missed her job there. She missed being a scholar.

She crumpled up her yogurt cup and tossed it into the recycling bin, then gave her spoon one last lick before slinging it into the sink. She stretched her arms high over her head and tilted her chair onto its back two legs, staring at the pipes criss-crossing the studio's open ceiling.

She didn't like to think about the library. Budget cuts plus her poor people skills got her fired from that job—*Lord, am I about to be fired again? From a coffeehouse this time!*—and until Zach had gotten past her defenses, she hadn't known what to do with herself.

She'd languished for weeks. To her dad's great displeasure, her Aunt Miranda had shown up in the aftermath of her firing and tried to pump some life back into her. Miranda had grabbed her by the arm, tossed her sorry ass into the shower, pulled the tags off some new little red number that was supposed to be a dress, and took her drinking and dancing. They had found some exclusive club and the bouncer had waved them right through.

How does Miranda even knew about these places? Cass wondered. *She doesn't even live in this state!*

The lights in the club had been dim and Cass had been able to feel the bass in her bones. A huge, ironic disco ball had presided over the dance floor. Miranda had ordered them a couple of drinks—nothing with umbrellas, just Scotch on the rocks. She had downed the first in one pull and asked for another. Cass had done the same.

The drinking part Cass was good at. The dancing part she was okay at. But the people part had been a disaster like always. Even half drunk, most guys had been too scared to talk to her. Or, if they had enough courage to try, they would get confused and disappointed once they had bought her a drink and tried to look deep into her wandering eye. Then they would make an excuse, step away, and never come back in her direction. Cass hadn't even been left with the consolation of thinking their excuses might not be lies.

"Whatever," she had slurred to her drink. "Screw them."

Still, she loved her aunt for trying. And, despite the blinding hangovers, a couple of nights out with Miranda had done her some good. What's more, Miranda's arrival fit a larger pattern. Ever since her mom had died, Miranda had shown a kind of sixth sense for knowing when Cass needed her most. Cass didn't doubt this would always be true.

Tonight, though—late at night, alone in her loft—she was on her own. She closed her dissertation, flipped it over, and slapped it down onto the table.

Enough! she thought.

She wanted to be done with this. She wanted to forget her failures. She wanted to move on with her life.

But she couldn't. In all her worrying tonight, she hadn't even touched the part that stung the most.

Her dad.

She missed her dad even more than she missed her work. She used to see him at the library almost every day. He would carve some time out of his schedule as head librarian and they would have lunch together in the university cafeteria while she shared the highlights from her latest research.

But in the months since she'd been fired from the library—since *her own dad* had fired her from her job at the library—she'd barely seen him at all.

How were they supposed to talk after that?

She felt like crying but didn't.

She flopped back onto her mattress and stuffed her head under her pillow instead.

She dreamed the rest of the night about books and relics.

6

Cass had a double shift the next day, from noon to closing. The sun was actually out for once—surprise!—so there weren't many customers. Business always slowed to a crawl when people weren't stuck inside, huddled around hot cups of coffee for warmth. But for Cass, all this really meant was that she had too much time on her hands to think about things she didn't want to think about. And after yesterday's episode with the manager, she didn't dare distract herself with her phone.

She tried to keep busy changing filters and straightening cups and wiping down tables and counters. She didn't mind the cleaning part of the job, it was definitely more her speed than the people part. But there was only so much to do on this front and, after a couple of hours, she was reduced to just leaning against the counter and staring out the front window, trying to guess the astrological signs of each person that walked by.

Her mom had taught her this game. They used to play at the bus stop while they waited.

"There are twelve signs of the Zodiac," her mom had said. "Each of the signs is ruled by a planet and each planet is associated with certain traits and characteristics."

Her mom seemed to know a lot about this kind of thing, and whenever she talked about anything "magical" there was always a glint in her eye that Cass didn't see otherwise. Her dad, though, wasn't a fan, so she and her mom only played these games when he wasn't around.

Cass had always been good at the game. She had a knack. Sometimes, as a party trick, she would guess people's signs. She would go around the table as fast as she could, pointing and naming everyone's signs until the whole table had dissolved in laughter, delighted by the fact that she wasn't just bluffing; she was right.

In the end, though, she felt more like her dad. She believed in history and scholarship and reason. She believed that life was short and filled with loss. She didn't believe in magic or monsters or gods. She didn't believe in things that went *bump* in the night.

Still, it was a fun game to play. Thinking about her mom, Cass tried to focus and zero-in on the people walking by.

A professional looking women in her early fifties: Gemini.

A dad in a hoodie with a baby in a stroller: Pisces and Taurus (the baby was a Taurus).

A homeless man: Scorpio.

An elderly lady in a velvet track suit: Aquarius.

She played for half an hour without a single customer coming in. She leaned against the counter and buried her head in her arms. *This day is never going to end.* She wiped the counter again, wishing Zach would show up already for his evening shift.

She needed to see a friendly face.

Just as she was thinking this, a man in his late twenties pushed through the door, letting in a gust of wind. He was tall with sandy hair and was dressed for Wall Street, not Oregon. He took a commanding look around the room and seemed pleased to find Java's Palace basically empty.

He smiled, unsurprised that things were going, as usual, just as he'd hoped.

Clearly a Leo, Cass thought to herself. *A banker? A hedge fund manager?*

"Can I help you?" she asked in her friendliest barista voice.

"Yes," he said. "And only you can. I didn't come for the coffee. I've come for you."

As he said it, the lines around his pale blue eyes crinkled in a way that *almost* succeeded in making that line not sound ridiculous. Still, Cass couldn't help but feel a little wave of electricity travel up her spine as she blushed.

"Uhhh, okay," she said, trying to keep her eyes down and her hands busy. "That's kind of weird. How do you even know who I am?"

"I need to speak with you about your dissertation," he continued in a hard-to-place accent. British? "And, believe it or not, the matter is quite urgent."

Cass didn't know what to say. She specialized in history and archeology, both fields where the term "urgent" meant something like "get back to me within a month." He wasn't putting her on, though. He wasn't lying. She was sure about that. He really did need to talk to her about her dissertation. But this made her more reluctant, not less, to actually talk to him.

What the hell is going on, Cass wondered. *I bomb out of my doctoral program and now I'm some kind of b-grade academic celebrity for nut jobs? Great.*

The man could tell she was skeptical.

"Please, Ms. Jones. I'm quite serious. I do need your help. And it *is* rather urgent."

As he said this, he reached out to take her hand and bobbed his head to meet her downcast eyes. His hand was strong and he wore a Harvard Business School ring. She was annoyed when he touched her hand, but she felt a little shock of connection when she met his eyes. Rather than getting flustered by her lazy eye or settling, eventually, on her strong eye as his point of reference, this man immediately, without missing a beat, looked directly into her weak eye.

"Please," he repeated.

She felt the pull of his request—to be valued, to talk about her work again, to talk about her work with *him* —but this was all too much. She knew he was telling the truth, but she didn't know why. And that why, always so opaque for her, worried her.

She decided to be firm.

"I already told you I'm not interested. I don't know who you are or what you want. But my work has been officially classified a disaster by the university and I don't take well to being badgered by anonymous texts from strangers."

Cass heard Zach bang through the door behind her, still tying his apron.

"Everything all right here, Cass?" Zach asked.

Mr. Harvard was confused by Cass's response and flustered by Zach's sudden appearance and protective posture. He withdrew his hand and stood up straight, more than a foot taller than Cass. She could tell he was not used to bumping into any kind of objections or road blocks. He was used to just getting what he wanted. Immediately.

Definitely a damn Leo, Cass thought.

"But I never—" the stranger began, recovering.

She cut him off. "If you don't need a coffee, then please leave. Now. My boss is going to come out here any minute; I'm already on thin ice, and you're going to get me fired."

She watched him realize that she was serious and, more, that he had misjudged the situation. He had misjudged her. Still, being a Leo, he would probably come back and start over again.

He hinted at a theatrical bow with a little wave of his hand, snapped his card onto the counter—Richard

York—and turned on his heel to leave, cell phone in hand.

Cass was surprised that he'd agreed to go so quickly. And, to be honest, part of her was sad to see him go. She was pleased, though, to feel the hostile, jealous vibe coming from Zach. It was a welcome consolation prize.

7

Java's Palace was dead the rest of the day. Only a handful of people wandered in over the next couple of hours and not a single one of them looked like a bronzed Olympic swimmer in a ten-thousand-dollar suit with an MBA from an Ivy League school. Not a single damn one.

Cass chatted a bit with Zach, but after the little incident with Mr. Harvard he seemed withdrawn and distracted, and spent most of his shift in the back reorganizing the supply room. Since they were working the evening shift their manager had already gone, and it was just the two of them.

A couple of times she heard Zach swearing like a sailor as he wrestled with boxes of styrofoam cups, but she didn't check on him. She just gave him some space. What happened between a man and his styrofoam cups wasn't any of her business. Plus, all the baristas at Java's lived by the same shared code: what happened in the stockroom, stayed in the stockroom. The stockroom was a sacred space.

Cass wasn't really in the mood to talk anyway. Like Zach, she felt distracted, her mind ping-ponging between thoughts about her dad, her dissertation, and Mr. Harvard. Though, given the unpleasant associations of the first two, her thoughts were tending toward Harvard.

She patted the front pocket of her jeans. She could feel his business card burning a hole in it.

She pulled it out and looked at it again. It was obviously expensive—heavy black backing with embossed white lettering—but it didn't contain any of the usual information. Just his name. It was like you were supposed to already know who he was and how to get in touch with him and, if you didn't, then you probably weren't supposed to.

She flipped the card over—nothing on the back. She smelled it. It bore the faint but distinct scent of pricey cologne. She thought about biting off a corner to see what it tasted like but decided that was just too weird.

Richard York, Richard York, Richard of York ... What kind of name was that, anyway? English royalty? Was his mom the duchess of something? It seemed like the kind of name you'd have if you were a leading member in some skull and bones Harvard cabal. Also, what about his first name, Richard? Did his friends call him "Dick" for short?

She didn't know. This whole thing was strange.

Had she been too abrupt? Had she been wrong about this guy? What if Dick *wasn't* a dick? Was there really something to her dissertation? Were people taking it seriously? Had she just shut the door on something that, at this low point in her life, she really needed, whether she wanted to admit it or not?

Pull yourself together Jones, or you're going to end up under that park bench fighting pigeons for bread crumbs like Zach predicted.

She put the business card back in her pocket, pleased to again feel its subtle burn against her thigh.

When Zach popped his head in to say it was time to close, Cass sent him home and promised to wipe everything down herself. She wanted to be alone.

Zach caught her vibe and didn't put up a fight. He grabbed his jacket and motorcycle helmet, gave her arm a squeeze, and headed out the door.

Once he was gone, Cass locked all the doors and got to work. She wiped down the counter and serving area first, then the tables. She flipped all the chairs onto the tables and swept the floors.

She gathered her stuff and was about to turn off the lights when she came to a decision. She pulled out her phone and reread the text from yesterday, the text that had started this whole thing and that she assumed was from Richard.

She could just text him. She had his number. She could just change her mind. She could simply arrange to meet him someplace safe and neutral and see what he had to say. She walked in a slow circle around the room and tried composing a message.

Changed my mind. Been thinking about your abs all day. Let's meet for drinks.

No. That was *not* the right approach here. She deleted the whole thing and tried again.

Changed my mind. Let's meet to talk more about what you're proposing. - C

After the aborted first draft, though, this tamer draft still sounded too skeezy to actually send.

"What you're proposing?" Am I expecting him to proposition me? Propose marriage? Good Lord! Which would be worse?

And now this little failed experiment in composing a text had her doubting her own motives. And motives, in the end, were the real sticking point. She could tell Mr. Richard York was being truthful with her, but she couldn't tell why. In addition to doubting her own motives, she couldn't tell the first thing about *his*.

She deleted the whole thing again and pocketed her phone.

I'll get back to you tomorrow, Dick, she thought.

She locked the door behind her and headed toward her car. She turned the corner, lost in her own thoughts, and was almost to her car, keys in hand, before she noticed three big guys in black leather with ominous postures waiting for her there.

Her first thought was: *Shit.*

Her second thought was: *Black leather? Seriously?*

Her third thought was, again: *Shit.*

But her fourth thought was more useful: *Swords. In the trunk.*

She decided to make the opening move.

"Hey guys," she said. "Mind getting off my car?"

The men stood up straight and gathered themselves.

"Ms. Jones?" the tallest asked.

Cass tightened her grip on her keys, slipping three of them between her fingers, improvising a set of sharp brass knuckles.

Go for their eyes and balls, she repeated to herself. *Eyes and balls. Eyes and balls.*

"Maybe," Cass answered. "Who's asking?"

"We are."

"And who, pray tell, are you?"

Eyes and balls.

"Well, Ms. Jones," the tall one said, his smile broadening to reveal a mouthful of sharp, brilliantly white teeth, "we're vampires."

Cass felt her lazy eye twitch and pull into focus. This guy was telling the truth. Or, at least, he *thought* he was.

8

"RIIIGHT. AND I'M the queen of England," Cass replied. "Tea, anyone?"

Cass had a bad feeling about this, but, for the moment at least, she decided she didn't really care what these men thought they were. All three had eyes and (presumably) balls. That was all that mattered for now.

The tall one signaled his two associates and they moved in tandem to grab Cass.

Cass dropped her bag and settled into a subtle defensive stance.

The side street where she'd parked was dark and quiet. Several of the street lights were out. It was late and there wasn't likely to be any traffic coming to her rescue. The air was cool and the incoming clouds signaled that rain, again, was on its way. Thunder rumbled in the distance.

"Who can I serve first, gentlemen?" Cass asked. "Do you take sugar or cream with your tea? Would you like a biscuit or crumpet to round things out?"

Neither of the men smiled. The one to her left moved first. He was at least a foot taller than she was and had more than a hundred pounds on her. Showing his own set of pointy white teeth, he lunged for her arms, hoping to quickly pin her and settle this whole thing with a minimum of fuss.

Cass was waiting.

In one smooth motion, she slipped her foot through the strap of her dropped bag and swung her leg through a powerful arc that sent the bag, heavy with books, crashing into the man's face, breaking his jaw and sending him reeling. He staggered backward, surprised, and spit out some bloody teeth into his hand. Blood and saliva dripped from his chin. He looked down at the teeth in his hand, then up at Cass in disbelief, and then back to the teeth in his hand. For a moment, Cass thought he was going to shrug off the blow, but then his knees buckled, his eyes rolled back into his head, and he collapsed onto the ground in a heap of black leather.

History books, one, she thought. *"Vampires,"* zero.

The leader, still hanging back, looked both surprised and amused.

The other guy, though, was not amused. He just looked angry. Cass could tell right away that she'd had her freebie. This guy was taking her seriously and he wouldn't make the same mistake as his friend.

He tried to circle around Cass but she was slippery, ducked a punch, and put some extra distance between them.

The guy sneered, shrugged his leather jacket, and feinted a couple of jabs at Cass's face.

Cass didn't fall for it, though. In fact, she never fell for feints. In the same way she could tell when someone was lying with words, she could tell when they were lying with their bodies. This gave her a serious advantage when she sparred because her power to instinctively tell feints from true blows gave her an almost prescient fighting style. She could take advantage of openings that, technically, weren't even open yet.

Still, this guy's length was a problem. She would have to step well inside his strike zone if she wanted to get anywhere near tagging him, while he could stay a step back and keep her within reach.

He threw a couple more punches that she successfully dodged until, sensing an opening, Cass stepped right through a blow, shorting him, and threw an uppercut of her own that connected. While he was still stunned, she jabbed with her keys straight for his eye.

Bingo.

She could feel the soft tissue burst and felt, for a moment, disgusted by the bloody mess she'd made. This guy would never see out of that eye again.

But black leather guy number two was an experienced fighter and he took advantage of her disgust and hesitation. Ignoring the pain, he threw a haymaker that, even when she saw it coming, she couldn't avoid. His fist slammed into the side of her face and her whole world exploded into stars. As Cass stumbled under the force of his blow, the man swept her leg, sent her sprawling to the ground, and moved immediately to deliver a flurry of game-ending kicks to her ribs.

Cass dropped her elbows to protect her side, squeezed her eyes shut, and curled into a ball.

She thought of her mom—would she see her again if she died? She thought of her dad—could he survive losing her *and* her mom? She thought of Zach. She thought of her dissertation. All these thoughts flashed through her mind as she braced herself.

Then she heard screaming.

"Aagghhh! What the—? Get off me, you damn cat!" the guy raged.

She stole a peek through her fingers and saw that an orange tabby—*her* orange tabby?—had attached itself to the guy's face like something straight out of *Alien*. His hands and already bloody face were getting shredded by the cat's razor sharp claws and teeth.

Cass hadn't seen her cat in days—*What the hell is Atlantis doing here?*—but she wasn't going to waste the chance he'd given her by wondering where he'd been or why he was here now. She got her arms under her for leverage and mule-kicked the guy right in the groin. He forgot about fending off the cat, grabbed his crotch, dropped to his knees, and started keening at an ungodly pitch.

Vampires, it turned out, *did* have balls.

As Atlantis jumped clear of the man's face, Cass moved to finish him off. She delivered a round-house kick to his head that knocked him flat and turned out his lights.

Cass was still seeing stars and half of her face was going to be one big bruise tomorrow. She could already feel it swelling.

She stood up slowly, rolled her neck, vertebrae cracking, and spit the blood from her mouth.

History books, one. House cat, one. Vampires, still zero. Now, where's that last guy?

The last guy was still leaning against her car, smiling. He greeted her victory with a mocking slow-clap that broke into laughter.

"Wow," he said. "Just ... wow. That was not what they said to expect. But I'm glad to have seen it. I'm glad you've got a little fight in you. This should be fun."

Lightning cracked somewhere nearby, thunder followed almost immediately, and rain started to fall. Fat drops pattered the pavement between Cass and the man.

Cass wiped the water from her face. She didn't feel any regret for hurting these assholes. They'd started it anyway. But she did feel something else, a kind of fire spreading from her heart out into the rest of her body, that she'd never felt before. It felt powerful. And she liked it—even as her own hungry response to that power worried her. This wasn't just adrenaline. This felt like something more. This felt like magic. This felt like her mom.

As the fire spread up her neck and across her face, everything seemed to slow down. Time itself seemed to slow down. Her lazy eye locked into focus and her cataract swirled for a moment before it burnt off entirely, like morning fog under the heat of a rising sun.

Cass breathed deeply. Her eyes burned like black coals.

For the first time in a long time, everything seemed clear. Everything in the world seemed sharp and well-defined.

The rain was falling heavily now and her clothes were already soaked. Cass peeled off her jacket. Her tight, black "The Future is Female" t-shirt clung to her torso. She could feel her socks squish in her shoes. She rolled a hairband off her wrist and pulled her black hair back into a wet ponytail.

"You never said," Cass yelled above the sound of the rain, "whether you wanted sugar and cream with that tea. It looks like we're out of cookies, though. Take that up with your friends."

The remaining guy smiled as the blood drained from his face making him, impossibly, even more pale then he already was. He cracked his knuckles and tossed his own leather jacket onto the hood of her car. His eyes turned albino pink and the veins and tendons in his neck and arms bulged. His fingernails looked more like claws. His whole body seemed to swell like he'd just pressed his "I'm Bane and now I'm going to break your back, Batman" button.

Shiiiit, Cass thought. *Shit. Shit. Shit.*

She considered running but knew she wouldn't make it far. No, her only hope was in the trunk of her old Volvo.

Maybe if she ran straight at him, screaming, he'd be frightened and she'd put him off balance?

She took another look at him now, his chest wide and heaving as he breathed heavily like something that had escaped from the zoo.

Uhhh, probably not, she thought.

In the end, he decided for her. With blazing speed, backlit by a crack of lightning, he rushed her, leading with his shoulder, looking to tackle her.

Normally, Cass wouldn't have stood a chance. But as he made his move, she felt the heat flare through her body again. With her eyes focused and her vision clear, time slowed to a crawl. Rather than ducking or trying to slip to the side, Cass took a running step toward the vampire, met him halfway, and vaulted neatly over his back, sending him sprawling.

Key fob still in hand, she popped the trunk of her car before she'd even landed. She took the landing in stride and, before the guy could even get to his feet, she was already pulling a sword from the trunk of her car.

Now who's in charge, asshole, she thought as she brandished her sword.

This last guy was back on his feet now. His eyes flashed with fear and anger when he saw the sword and she grinned back at him.

But this only lasted a moment before *he* started laughing.

What the hell?

Case looked down at the sword in her hand.

It was a padded practice sword.

What was she going to do, tickle him with it?

The guy was on top of her in the blink of an eye, batting the sword from her hand and pinning her against the rear of her car. He seemed even larger than he had been a moment before. She tried to knee him in the balls but he blocked her blow.

His teeth shone in the dark and he leaned in toward her. Was he going to bite her?

He really does think he's a vampire! What the hell?!

Cass knew she only had a moment left to act. Shifting all her weight, she stomped on his foot, knocking him off balance, and then used that momentum to flip their positions. Now he was pinned against the back of her car, leaning back into the open space of her trunk. With one hand on his throat, Cass reached over him and grabbed the trunk lid. She smashed the trunk lid down onto his face again and again.

That's gonna leave a mark.

And it did. But it didn't seem to slow him down. It only seemed to make him angrier.

He roared back at her and, as she leaned past him to root in the trunk for some other kind of weapon, he tossed her into the air. Cass flew backwards and landed hard on her back, knocking the wind out of her.

The guy moved to pin her to the ground before she could recover but froze mid-stride. His eyes were locked on her right hand.

Case had found what she was looking for in the trunk: a razor sharp katana.

In one smooth motion, Cass flipped back onto her feet. Time slowed even more. The guy didn't even have time to react. Swinging the sword through a tight round, she screamed at the top of her lungs and then, with one decisive stroke, separated the man's head from his body.

She squinted her eyes and turned away, expecting blood to jet everywhere. But, instead, the man just burst into a cloud of chalky ash. In this gale, what was left of him was gone before she could register what had happened.

Cass blinked, struggling to make sense of what had just happened.

"Huh," Cass said to herself out loud. "I guess they really were vampires."

As quickly as it had come, Cass felt all the heat and strength drain right out of her. It was like someone had pulled the plug from the bottom of the tub.

She dropped to her hands and knees in the middle of the street. She felt sick. The rain was still pouring.

The other two vampires had, in the meantime, disappeared entirely.

Cass felt her vision cloud and her weak eye lose focus.

But in that moment, just before her eye returned entirely to normal, something else happened: time stopped entirely. It was like she'd slid sideways, for just an instant, outside the normal flow of time. In that frozen moment, Cass had a vision of her mother. Or, rather, Cass had a vision in which she *was* her mother.

She saw, from her mother's perspective, that bright summer morning when the two of them had sat on ten-year-old Cass's bed and her mother had squeezed her hand and given her the pendant that she wore to this day. Her mother made her swear—literally, swear with an oath—to care for this pendant with her life. At the time, Cass had been enthralled by the necklace. But seeing this scene from her mom's perspective, she could see what she'd taken for granted at the time. She could feel how much her mom loved and trusted her. She could feel the strength of her hand. She could feel how deep her hopes ran for her.

And then the vision ended.

Time started again.

And Cass was alone in the middle of the wet street, clutching her pendant in one hand, crying.

9

CASS STARTED HER car, turned on the windshield wipers, and cranked the heat all the way up. It would take a couple minutes, though, before any warmth actually materialized. The rain pounded on her roof. She couldn't see more than a few yards down the street. Waiting for the heat, Cass revved her engine and sat shivering in her seat, teeth chattering, goosebumps pimpling her skin from head to toe.

She dried her eyes, took a deep breath, and tried to get a grip on what had just happened.

Her life had just broken into two pieces—the before and the after. Everything that happened now would be "after." Nothing would ever be the same. As much she *already* pined for the boring simplicity of the afternoon shift she'd spent guessing people's astrological signs, there was no going back.

She could never go back.

She'd seen what those things were—call them vampires or whatever you want, they weren't human—and, even more decisively, she'd *felt* what had happened to *her*.

A door deep inside of her heart—a door that had been there her entire life, but locked—was now unlocked. That door stood wide open and she could feel the far side of it calling to her, inviting her to step beyond what she had thought she was and into this other world. Into the world of magic.

Now that she could hear the call so clearly, she realized that she'd heard this voice whispering to her all her life. For a long time, she'd thought the whispers were just a fragment of her mother's memory, an illusion generated by her own mourning. Even if that was partly true, it clearly wasn't the whole story.

Whatever was happening to her, it was real.

But even if she could no longer ignore or dismiss the call, she still didn't feel ready to cross that threshold. The door was open and unlocked—she couldn't do anything about that—but *she* would decide if and when she stepped through it.

Warm air started to flow through the air vents. She adjusted them so that every vent in the car was pointing squarely at her and rubbed her hands in front of them.

Heat was the first order of business. But she also needed to talk to someone. She needed to not be alone with this.

She tried to wrestle her phone out of her wet jeans and pulled out Mr. Harvard's business card instead. It was dry as a bone and didn't have a single wrinkle.

What the hell is this thing made out of?

She pinged the card with a flick of her finger.

Is this paper-thin titanium? How rich is this guy?

She couldn't worry about that now. She tossed the card onto the passenger seat and tried again for her phone. The phone's screen was cracked and some moisture fogged the glass from the inside, but it worked when she turned it on.

She thought about calling her dad. But if she was going to repair that bridge, this didn't seem like the place to start.

That really only left Zach. Being short on people skills and short on friends didn't leave her with many options.

She pulled her legs up onto the driver's seat, hugged her knees, double-checked that the heat was cranked all the way up, and dialed Zach.

He answered on the first ring.

"What's wrong? Are you okay, Cass?"

How did Zach already know something was wrong? Was he sitting on his phone, waiting for me to call? Should I be flattered or worried?

"What …? How did you …?"

"Cass, we're friends and I'm here for you. But I can count on one hand—hell, I don't even have to *use* any hands—the number of times you've ever called me just to chat: zero. If you're calling now, it must be important."

"Yeah, I … I don't really know where to begin. I … I was attacked—"

Zach cut her off. "Cass, are you okay? Are you hurt? Where are you?"

"I'm okay," she said, fingering the bruised side of her face. "I'm okay. I took care of it." She paused, then smiled wearily. "You should see the other guys."

"Cass! What!"

"It's not just this, though. Weird shit has been happening for the past twenty-four hours. Even weirder than normal. It started with this anonymous text yesterday asking about my dissertation, then that guy came into the coffeehouse today looking for me and asking about my research, and then these three sleazy dudes were waiting for me tonight at my car after I'd locked up the shop—"

"Wait, that *guy* from earlier today, the smug douche bag in the suit, he's part of this? I'll beat him to a pulp —"

"Hold on there cowboy," Cass replied. "Simmer down. That guy is definitely *part* of this weirdness but these dudes from tonight don't seem like his style. That guy in the suit would just buy me, not kidnap me."

Cass tried to fill in more of the details for Zach, but the more she said and the weirder her story got, the more agitated he became.

"It's not safe out there, Cass," he argued. "It's not safe for you to be alone right now. Come over to my place. I'll make up the couch for you. I'll watch out for you tonight."

The offer was appealing, even if the idea of Zach hurting (or protecting) *anyone* seemed ridiculous. How much protecting did she need, anyway? She'd just killed a vampire herself, after all! Really, she should be smart and keep *him* out of harm's way.

Once this thought occurred to her, she knew she couldn't go over there, much as part of her wanted to. Zach didn't deserve to be dragged into this.

"I can't. I'm … I'm going to see my dad," she lied. "But I'll catch up with you tomorrow."

Before Zach could say anything else, she hung up.

She popped the car into gear and took off. The rain was tapering off and it didn't take long to get home. This time of night, parking wasn't a problem and all the cars left out on her street looked like hers: dinged hand-me-downs from parents.

But tonight something on her street was painfully, obviously different. A shiny black Model X Tesla was parked in front of the Thai restaurant. The neon blue of the store's "noodles" sign reflected cleanly off the car's sweeping glass roof.

Cass pulled quietly into a spot across the street and cut the engine.

She took a closer look. Nobody was waiting for her in the car. That was good.

But the outer door leading up to her apartment was open.

She was positive she'd locked it this morning.

10

Cass drove around the block and parked out of sight. She opened the car door, got out, and turned to go, but then thought better of leaving empty handed. She leaned back into the car, reached across the gearshift, and snagged her katana. For good measure, she also grabbed Richard York's business card from the passenger seat and slid it back into her pocket. It still burned cooly against her thigh.

Focus, Jones, she told herself. *Focus*.

Sword in hand, she felt ridiculous creeping around the corner of her own building, trying to stick to the shadows. What was she, a ninja now?

She reached the door at the base of the stairs leading to her apartment. It was still ajar. She used her foot to swing it wide open. She decided to try being strong and decisive and jumped into the doorway with her sword raised. She saw something dark move on the stairs and a jolt of fear shot through her. She almost took a swing with her sword before she caught herself. She was so jumpy she'd almost cut the head off her own shadow.

Smooth move, ex-lax. If anyone needs help killing their own shadow, you'll be ready. Anything worse than that, though, and you'll both be in real trouble.

She shook her head, disgusted with herself, and started up the wooden stairs. She stayed close to the wall, sticking to the sides of the stairs to avoid making any unnecessary noise. Ten quiet steps later, she reached the landing outside her apartment door. Like the door downstairs, this door was also almost shut, but not quite. She could see that the latch hadn't engaged.

Cass took a deep breath and tried to steel herself for whatever came next. She tried to feel around in her chest for some of that magic heat and focus that had kicked in earlier, saving her butt, but the only thing she found there now was her own heart knocking with fear against her rib cage.

On three, she told herself.

One.

Two.

Four!

She skipped right past three in order surprise both herself and whoever was on the other side of the door. She gave the door a solid kick that sent it banging open so hard it almost bounced closed again before she could get through it. She felt even more ridiculous when it rebounded a final time and hit her on the ass.

She didn't know whether to laugh or cry. She stifled both.

Dear God in heaven, I don't know if you're listening, or if you even exist, but I could use some help here. Please? Amen.

The interior of the apartment was pitch black. The lights were off and the blinds were drawn.

"Hello, Cassandra," a disembodied voice said quietly from the heart of the darkness.

Cass almost jumped but forced herself into a defensive posture instead, her sword extended in front of her. She closed her eyes and tried to feel her way out into the rest of the room, Jedi-style, with only her other senses. It was so dark she wasn't going to see anything anyway.

It *felt* like there was just one person, a man, sitting near the far wall.

"Cassandra," the voice intoned again.

Who the hell calls me Cassandra? she wondered. *Not even my dad calls me Cassandra.*

Then, before she had a chance to call on any other fledgling Jedi skills, the man flicked on the living room lamp.

Richard York was sitting on her old yellow couch. He smiled thinly when he saw her sword. Her cat, Atlantis, was sitting on his lap, purring.

"I hope you don't mind," he said. "I made myself at home. It seemed rude to wait outside when your cat invited me in. He was so friendly I just followed him right up the stairs and through your front door."

She cocked her eyebrow at him.

"Does your cat have his own key?" he asked, half joking, scratching Atlantis behind the ears. He grinned, pleased with himself.

"Oh, and I found something else. These," he said, "must be yours."

With a touch of drama, he slowly pulled (her?) black bra out from between the couch cushions. He dangled the lace in the air with one hand, cocking his own eyebrow, and then opened his other hand, revealing thirty-seven cents.

Cass was not amused, even if she couldn't avoid blushing.

"Nice trick, asshole," Cass snapped without lowering her sword. "First, put the cat down. Now."

Without waiting for Richard to make a move, Atlantis jumped down of his own accord. When the cat hit the floor, he stopped for a moment and looked straight at Cass. And winked. Then he disappeared behind the couch.

What the ... Did my cat just wink at me?

"Second, who are you and why are you here?"

"I already tried to tell you earlier today," Richard said. "I represent a powerful group of investors who are in need of your ... unique ... and impressive set of skills."

He was still dangling the bra in the air between them.

He looked at the bra and then back at her, as if he were trying to decide whether it fit.

"Put that damn thing down, already" Cass barked, pointing with her sword.

Richard smiled and, with a hint of regret, dutifully complied, draping it over the arm of the couch.

"I already told you," Cass continued, "I'm not interested in the Kool-Aid you're selling. I can ruin my own life. I don't need any expensive, outside help from you."

"I believe you," he said. "Though I suspect that, with a little help from me, you might be able to ruin your life in a much more interesting way. I'm offering you a chance to step off the sidelines and get in the game. I'm offering you the chance to put your life's work to the test."

He waited a beat, holding her gaze, looking right into her weak eye again.

"I'm offering you the chance to find out *if you're right*. And, unless I'm completely mistaken, I don't believe you're capable of turning that offer down."

Cass's grip on her sword relaxed and she could feel her resolve cracking.

He was telling the truth. He was making a serious offer.

And he was telling the truth about her. This *was* what she wanted, deep down: the chance to prove that she was right. Not just to show her dissertation committee or colleagues that she was right but, especially, to prove something to her dad. To prove to her dad, once and for all, that she (and her mom) were *right*.

She lowered the sword to her side.

Seeing her relax, Richard sank back into the couch. Even if Cass had trouble reading people, it was obvious that Richard didn't have any trouble reading her. He had her pegged.

"Excellent," he said. "Excellent. And, while we have a moment, I think these might also be yours." And with that, he pulled a tiny black thong out from between the couch cushions.

Whatever the story was with the bra, Cass was certain that *these*, at least, were *not* hers.

But before she could blush or get angry or feel that business card melt a hole through her pocket, the scene completely imploded as Zach burst through her apartment door, also taking a shot from the rebounding door, brandishing a large wooden cross and yelling "Get thee behind me, Satan!" or something along those lines.

He was in attack-mode, but stopped dead in his tracks when he, Richard, and Cass all simultaneously locked eyes on the panties still swinging gently from the end of Richard's finger.

11

WHILE EVERYONE WAS distracted by the thong, Atlantis made a break for the door. The only one who noticed was Cass. One moment the cat was hidden behind the couch, the next an orange patch of fur streaked across the room and out the open door, and then—poof—Atlantis was lost again. Who knew when she'd see him. The cat kept his own counsel.

Zach and Richard, though, kept their steely gazes glued to the thong, testing each other—neither seemed to want to be the first to look away and lose face.

"Grow up, boys," Cass said as she snatched the panties from the end of Richard's finger and stuffed them into her back pocket. "We've got real problems to worry about."

With the spell broken, Zach stepped protectively between Cass and Richard, waving the cross in Richard's direction while looking back over his shoulder to see if Cass was okay.

He commanded the room in a way Cass had never seen before. His normal slouch and laid-back attitude had evaporated. His shoulders were square and he seemed an inch or two taller. His biceps strained against the sleeves of his t-shirt.

Who the hell is this guy? Cass wondered. *What happened to mild-mannered Zachary Riviera? Does Zach have a secret identity? Is he a crime-fighting vigilante by night? Wait, is Zach Batman!?*

"You, stay right there," Zach ordered, pointing the cross at Richard.

Richard just raised his hands in mock surrender and smiled, though Cass could have sworn he looked more uncomfortable then he was letting on.

"Cass, are you okay?" Zach asked, turning his attention back to her.

His searching look swept up from Cass's feet and toward her face, cataloguing any signs of distress or injury. He looked mostly relieved until his eyes reached her face and he got a good look at the deep black bruise blooming across her cheek. An expression overtook him that she'd never seen before. He was so easy-going, that she didn't know he *could* get angry. The fury took hold of him in an instant and made him almost unrecognizable.

Zach spun back toward Richard.

"I'll kill you," he whispered with an intensity that made his words seem more like an actual promise than an idle threat.

A look of real worry flashed across Richard's face.

Zach moved fast to cross the distance between them. Richard was on his feet in one preternaturally smooth movement. But Cass was quickest of all. She wedged her sword into the wooden floor, grabbed Zach in a bear hug, and shouted, "Stop, Zach! Stop! It wasn't him, it doesn't have anything to do with him—"

Zach tried to shrug her off, struggling and unconvinced, until Cass brushed the lobe of his ear with her bottom lip as she whispered his name just loud enough for him to hear. "Shhh, Zach ... shhh."

Cass felt the fight drain out of Zach as quickly as it had come.

"I'm okay," Cass whispered. "I'm okay. In fact, something has changed. I may be a little bruised but, really, I feel *more* than okay. I feel better than I have in a long time. I feel ... plugged-in."

Zach twisted around and returned her hug, holding her head close against his chest, still keeping one eye on Richard.

"It's not that simple, Cass," Zach said, holding her a couple of beats too long before awkwardly letting her go. "Even if he didn't hit you himself, this guy is hip-deep in whatever shit you stumbled into tonight."

Cass knew there was something to what Zach was saying. Clearly, all these weird events were linked. She just wasn't sure how.

She was about to grant the point when she looked down at Zach's hand and it clicked in her mind that Zach hadn't brought a gun or a sword or baseball bat with him when he'd thought she was in danger.

He'd brought a cross.

"Zach, uhhhh, why are you holding a cross?"

She'd told him about the attack, and she'd told him that the men had been creepy, but she hadn't told him she'd cut someone's head off. And she definitely hadn't used the word "vampire."

Zach looked confused for a moment, seemingly unsure of how to respond.

"What, this old thing?" he tried. "It was just laying around my apartment. I've got dozens of them. It's just the first thing I grabbed when I ran out the door. It doesn't mean anything at all."

Cass tapped her foot and let him dig his own hole deeper.

"Dozens of them, huh. Just laying around your apartment," Cass said.

"Yeeaaah," Zach stammered. "Yeah, you know how some people collect little decorative spoons or vintage comic books or Beanie Babies? I collect, uhh, weapons-grade crosses?"

Cass reached out and took his free hand in hers, looking him straight in the eye.

"Zach," she said gently, "that's bullshit. How did you know to bring a cross? How did you know that the low-lifes I ran into tonight were—" She choked on the word for a moment, but then decided just to own it. "Vampires?"

Zach didn't balk at this description. He looked back at Richard. Richard's interest had perked up but, even so, he didn't blanch either. Surprisingly, no one seemed surprised that vampires were now part of the conversation.

"Cass, I promise to explain this all to you when we have time," Zach stalled, squeezing her hand. "But we've got to deal with something else first. Those guys from earlier aren't your only problem."

Zach extended the hand holding the cross in Richard's direction.

"This asshole is a vampire, too. Every time I wave the cross at this guy, he flinches."

For effect, Zach waved the cross in Richard's face and Cass thought she could detect a visible effort on Richard's part to *not* flinch or hiss or whatever a vampire would do. But, she wondered, would she act any different if someone were brandishing a cross in her face?

"Cass, I realize you've had a rough night," Richard broke in, "but that's ridiculous. I'm not like whatever you saw earlier tonight. You're not taking this seriously, are you? I came here looking for your *help*, not to hurt you."

Zach bristled at this denial and Richard responded in kind. Before things could get out of hand again, Cass took Zach by the arm and led him out onto the landing.

"Zach," Cass said.

Zach was still glaring at Richard through the doorway.

"Zach, over here, man." Cass snapped her fingers in front of his face. "Thank you for coming tonight. It means a lot to me. But I've got a *lot* to process and all this macho posturing isn't helping. I need you to give me a little space to figure things out. Call me in the morning. We'll talk, meet up, whatever. But give me a moment. I can handle this guy. And he's not going to tell me what I need to know if you're here … looming. I need to find out what this is all about."

Zach was still shooting laser-eyes at Richard—*What was he, Superman, not Batman? Clark Kent did seem like a better fit. Zach was no billionaire playboy, that's for sure* —but she watched his gaze shift back and forth a couple of times between Richard, the sword wedged in the floor, and Cass's battered practice dummy. He knew she could take care of herself.

"Alright," he relented. "Alright. But I'm calling first thing in the morning. And I'll be here again in a minute if you need me."

Cass nodded in agreement.

"Yes, yes, of course. I'll text you if anything happens."

"And you have to keep this," Zach said, tucking the front of her damp t-shirt into her jeans with two fingers and slipping his cross through a gap in her belt.

"Fine," she said, rolling her eyes. She gave him a gentle push. "Now *goooo* already."

Once Zach was gone, she shut the door, pulled the cross from her belt, and clapped it down on the counter.

Richard looked relieved.

"Now, Mr. York, *why* are you here in the first place. What, exactly, do you want from me?"

"Well …" he started, unable to keep that playful glint out his eye.

"For real," Cass snapped.

"I need you, Cassandra."

"For what?"

"There's a race underway," he started, "to find the One True Cross. And I believe you're the only one who actually knows how to do it."

12

"YOUR WORK IS brilliant," Richard said.

They were sitting at Cass's kitchen table with documents, maps, and photographs strewn about. The room was lit by a single floor lamp that left the loft's high ceilings in shadow. It was late. Coffee was brewing. Cass had slipped into dry jeans and a warm sweater. Richard's suit coat was draped neatly over the back of his chair, his tie loose, his shirtsleeves rolled up.

"Here. Look here," he said, pointing at a grainy photograph. "This is what I'm talking about."

Cass leaned in and squinted for a closer look. From Richard's open collar, she caught the faint scent of the same cologne that had clung to his business card. It smelled better—and even more expensive—on him. She couldn't make out, though, what he was pointing at.

"I've got a cleaner digital image of this same photo," she said. She kicked back from the table and rolled across the room in her chair toward her work desk. She unplugged her laptop and scooted back to the table. She flipped the screen open and found the file.

"Here," she said.

"Yes, this is it. Look right here." Richard pointed with his finger to an ancient fragment of wood, his other hand resting on the back of her chair. "Take a close look at the unusual texture and the growth pattern."

"I still can't quite make out the details," Cass replied.

"Let me try to enlarge the image," Richard said assertively. He pulled her laptop closer to him and then —didn't really know what to do.

"Hmmm," he frowned, like he'd been confronted with some artifact from the future.

Cass tossed her head back and laughed.

"Mr. Big Shot doesn't know how to enlarge a photo? What, were you born in the fifteenth century?" she joked.

He squirmed a little in his seat.

Had that last bit hit too close to home? Was he older than he looked? How much older than me is he? Do I care?

"Well …" he started.

She laughed again.

"I must confess," he continued, "I am a bit of a luddite. I'm a damn genius when it comes to the math that makes the world of finance turn, but these infernal machines … I've never really gotten the hang of them."

He threw up his hands.

She liked the fact that, apparently, he had a weak spot.

She easily zoomed in on the photo and saw immediately what he had wanted to show her.

Damn, Cass thought to herself, *he really knows what he's talking about.*

"I see it," she said, not quite keeping the note of excitement out of her voice, "I see it."

In the end, Richard's pitch was simple. The group he represented was deeply committed to recovering every remaining piece of the One True Cross. Their motives varied, but money was no object and they all believed that the fragments had more than historical value. Richard personally oversaw the working group tasked with the day to day business of searching for fragments. Reviewing her published research had sparked an idea for him, but he needed her help to fill in the blanks.

"Cassandra, we're not the only ones searching for these fragments. You got a taste tonight of what the bad guys look like and you know their hearts are black. Time is running out and we need you. The *good guys* need you."

Cass nodded, staring at the table top, reluctant to meet his eyes. She ran her fingers through her jet black hair.

Her life hadn't been easy, but tonight had been different. She'd never seen real evil before tonight. And, too, before tonight she'd never felt the kind of power connected with vanquishing it. She'd liked the feel of the sword in her hand. And she'd been energized by the moment of deep connection with her mother. She was frightened and exhilarated by the door that had opened in her heart.

What had she been training and studying for all her life, if not this?

Her dissertation was the key.

She'd used a cross-section of historical and literary texts to form a hypothesis about timber growth patterns in the areas where early Christians lived. Then, working from those patterns, she'd mapped the types of wood composing various relics and looked for anomalies. The fragments that fell within the right historical frame but failed to fit the larger material pattern were the prize. They were the potential pieces of the One True Cross on which—as Christians claimed—God himself had died.

She got up from the table, wandered over to her practice dummy, and half-heartedly delivered the opening series of blows in a complicated routine. Richard leaned back in his chair to watch.

She could feel her mind waver like a candle, weighing the pros and cons. She thought about her dad, wondered what he would think, and struck a wooden arm with enough force to rattle the whole dummy. She thought about her mom and wondered what she would want her to do. In truth, a big part of Cass just wanted to forget the whole thing and go back to selling coffee or working in a library. She yearned for the quiet. She was hungry for silence.

But when Richard gently said her name—"Cassandra"—breaking the silence, she admitted to herself what she had already known was true: there was no going back.

"I'll do what I can," she decided. "I'll at least get you started. But I can't offer you the kind of help you'll need from a desk in a library. I'll have to be present, in person, to sort the archeological, architectural, and literary clues that may be embedded in any prospective site."

"Done," Richard eagerly replied.

"And I'll need the kind of sophisticated lab support that grad students can't afford in order to analyze the fragments of wood."

"The lab support you need is already up and running."

"Anything else?"

"And I need you to trust me."

Richard extended his hand.

"I trust you," he said.

She took his hand, her small hand disappearing in his, and they shook on it.

"Let's go, then. Our plane is waiting." Richard said as he stood, slipped his coat back on, and pulled the keys from his pocket.

"Wait, our *what*?" Cass asked.

"You're in the big leagues, now, Miss Jones. Grab a change of clothes and whatever research you need. We'll be off the ground within the hour."

Cass stuffed some clothes and her laptop into a bag. All of her research materials were already in the cloud.

She paused at the door on her way out. Richard was already waiting at the bottom of the stairs. She felt like she was forgetting something.

Her sword.

She sheathed the katana and slung it over her shoulder, then slipped Zach's cross into her bag as well. Anything else? Atlantis would be on his own for a while, but when wasn't he? He'd be fine. And she'd call Zach from the plane and try to explain. Better to do that with a little distance between them.

She stepped through the door and locked it behind her.

No going back now, Jones. No going back.

Cass glanced up at the stairwell window. The evening's earlier storms had cleared, leaving behind a calm night sky. That seemed like as good an omen as any. She jogged down the stairs and in seconds they were both out the door, headed for the Model X.

But as soon as they were out the door her weak eye started to twitch and burn.

A dozen or so angry looking vampires, men and women, stepped out of the shadows and into the street.

13

THESE VAMPIRES LOOKED like they'd been briefed. Cass wouldn't be catching this group with their guard down. Some of the men were just wearing ironic t-shirts and skinny jeans—hipster vampire casual?—but *all* of the women were wearing tight black leather pants, corsets, jackets, etc.

Come on, ladies! Cass thought. *Seriously? Was there an enforced vampire dress code? Was feminism all for nought? In this humidity, that leather must squeak and chafe with every step.*

There was no talking this time, no preliminary banter. The vampires immediately started to circle around, hemming them in.

Cass could hear Richard swearing under his breath. She could feel her eye clearing and focusing, the cloudiness dissolving, a fire radiating from her bones. She dropped her bag and drew her sword. It felt true in her hand. Time slowed just a hair. Everything seemed sharply defined.

A woman signaled several of the group to position themselves between Cass and Richard and the car. She was apparently the leader. That made sense. Her pants seemed the tightest and, too, her corset seemed the bustiest.

Are those real? Cass couldn't stop herself from wondering and then gently shook her head. *No way. No damn way.*

She noticed that Richard had noticed, too. She couldn't say for sure, but the look in his eye seemed less skeptical—or, at least, less judgmental.

The group was basically in position now. Cass and Richard had their backs to the storefront. The vampires were just waiting for the signal.

The woman took one step forward. Her leather audibly squeaked as she moved and Cass was *sure* she saw her stifle a wince when her thighs rubbed together.

Ha! I knew it! Get some baby powder, asshole!

The woman gave the signal and the vampires closest to Cass and Richard leapt into action.

Cass wondered for a moment how she could possibly protect both herself *and* Richard from a dozen vampires. But when a vampire launched himself toward them, Richard plucked him out the air, grabbing him by the throat, and slammed him onto the pavement. She could hear the poor guy's vertebrae crackle as Richard twisted his head and broke his neck. She didn't know if you could kill a vampire that way, but he seemed dealt with for the moment.

Okaaaay, note to self: Richard can hold his own.

Cass needed to focus on her own problems. Two had already zeroed in on her, but they were leery of her sword. One made a move and Cass relieved him of his arm, blood spraying everywhere. The other angled in from the side but, as Cass exhaled, time slowed a fraction more. Still following through from her initial stroke, she spun on her heel and her blade passed cleanly through his neck. Before his head could roll, the vampire dissolved in a shower of ashy dust.

Cass and Richard were back to back now, facing opposite directions. The remaining vampires weighed their approach. The woman popping out of her corset didn't seem pleased with how things had started.

"Cass," Richard whispered. He reached back with his hand and felt for hers. "Do *you* trust *me*?"

Cass hesitated. Did she? She doubted that "trust" was the right word. But the truth seemed beside the point at the moment. Even if she didn't trust him, she *needed* him.

"Yes," she lied. "I trust you."

As soon as she said it, she knew it had been a mistake.

Her sword felt less true in her hand, her feet less steady, and the fire in her bones cooled.

Richard squeezed her hand.

"On two, toss me your sword."

He let go of her hand as the vampires between them and the car made their move.

"One," Richard said and pushed a button on his key fob, firing up the car's engine and blinding several vampires with the car's LED headlamps.

"Two," he said, pushing a second button on his fob that popped the car's gull-wing doors, cracking a vampire in the back of the head, sending him stumbling.

Cass tossed her sword to him, handle first. Richard snatched it cleanly out of the air, took off another vampire's head in one smooth stroke—poof!—and grabbed the now open car door with his other hand, smashing it down on the already dazed vampire's head.

Cass was impressed, but this wasn't going to be enough.

The others made their move.

There were too many of them.

And Cass wasn't strong enough or quick enough. Her connection to the strength she needed now felt weak and spotty—like she had one bar at best.

One of the female vampires leapt onto Richard's back while a second one wrenched the sword from his hand. At the same time a vampire tackled her from behind. As her knees buckled, the queen bee herself crash-landed on Cass's chest, doubling her over backwards. She hit the sidewalk hard.

Out of the corner of her eye, she could see Richard struggling to get the woman off his back, spinning in circles. Her sharp teeth were bared, her arms squeezing tight around his neck. His face was bright red. He tried to ram her against the brick wall, but misjudged his position. Instead, he smashed her into the storefront window of the noodle place, shattering the glass and propelling them both into the restaurant's interior.

Cass was in trouble, too.

"You're mine!" the woman screamed, pinning Cass to the ground.

The woman leaned in close and Cass wasn't sure if the woman intended to tear out her throat or—the corset looked like it had reached its breaking point—smother her to death.

Shit! Cass thought to herself. *Those things have been weaponized!*

Either way, Cass struggled futilely beneath the woman's leather-clad weight, her copper-scented breath hot on Cass's neck.

This is it.

This is the end.

Is my life going to flash before my eyes now, or what?

But just as the women went in for the kill, her eyes locked on the pendant around Cass's neck and she froze. A look of horror contorted her face.

Then, from nowhere, a clap of thunder shook the ground. Cass looked into the clear night sky in bewilderment. *What? Where did that come from?* But before she could take advantage of the opening, the thunder was followed by a crackling bolt of lightning that slammed into the queen bee, lifted her off Cass and pinned her to the brick wall, reducing her to ash.

All at once, every pair of eyes, vampire or human, turned to see where that bolt of energy had come from.

A petite, dark-haired women in stilettos stood in the street about ten feet away, ozone-scented smoke still rising from her hands.

"Get off her, you bitch," she snarled.

"Aunt Miranda?" Cass asked, still flattened on the sidewalk, incredulous.

"I've always wanted to say that," Miranda smiled and winked at Cass.

14

"HUH," CASS SAID out loud—her eyebrow raised, her ears still ringing—as her mind ground to a halt.

In many ways, it was easier to digest the existence of vampires than the fact that her favorite aunt had just shot green lightning out the end of her well-manicured fingertips. What next? Was her stodgy, "let's be rational about this" dad going to reveal himself as a werewolf?

Pull yourself together, Jones. You're not out of the woods yet.

Through the restaurant's shattered window, Cass could see Richard still struggling with the vampire that had attached herself to his back. They rolled through broken glass, knocking over chairs and tables as he tried to break her grip and peel her off. His suit was in tatters and he'd lost an Italian loafer somewhere along the way.

Miranda, on the other hand, looked like she was in complete control. And smiling.

Before Cass could catch her breath, Miranda clapped her hands together again with enough force to shake the ground—this must have been the "thunder" Cass had originally heard—and shaped a lime-tinged ball of light in her hands that, with obvious satisfaction, she sent crackling in three different directions, reducing three more vampires to piles of ash.

Despite the bravado, Cass could see that Miranda was not going to be able to keep this up. After that last effort, she could already see the blood draining from Miranda's face, and her hands were visibly shaking. Whatever she was doing and however she was doing it, the effort was draining her.

Cass rolled back to her feet and snatched up her sword from where Richard had dropped it. She wavered for a second, her vision cloudy. She almost leaned against the car for support but steeled herself to put on the kind of intimidating front that Miranda was still working to project.

Richard had struggled to his knees, the vampire still hanging like a millstone around his neck. With his feet under him, he reached behind his back with both hands, grabbed the woman by the waist, and then, summoning what strength he had left, let out a deep bellow and tossed her over his head and into a glass display case. The crash was horrific. The vampire was impaled on the case's jagged edge, blood foaming from her mouth.

The handful of remaining assailants took a hard look at Miranda, glanced at Cass with her sword, and took off running.

Cass couldn't believe it: they'd survived.

Richard was breathing heavily, face crimson, head bowed. He held out his hand to Cass.

Does he want to hold hands again? Now? In front of her aunt? And a half-dead vampire?

She hesitated.

"Cass," he said softly, shaking his head a little, pointing with his index finger, "sword."

Ahhh, yes. Right. Sword, she thought to herself.

She handed him the sword. He limped over to the display case, blood dripping from his knee, and cut off the vampire's head.

Ash.

"Thank you," he said politely, returning her sword, smoothing his blond hair, and straightening his tie.

Miranda looked ready to collapse in the middle of street.

Cass looked at Miranda and then at Richard. She felt a deep affection for both of them. Shared death and suffering and all that. Then she bent over, hands on her knees, and vomited into the gutter.

Richard gently touched her back, wiped tears from her eyes, and held her by the shoulders until the convulsions passed.

Miranda was still trying to pull herself together. When she was finally steady enough, she looked up to see Richard tenderly steadying Cass.

With this a deep, black anger flared across Miranda's face, as if she'd suddenly remembered why she was here in the first place.

She pointed at Richard, a wisp of smoke curling upward from the end of her fingertip.

"You," she spat at Richard. "Get your hands off her. Now. Or I'll fry your bloodsucking ass."

15

MIRANDA MEANT IT. And Cass believed her. She *would* fry his blood-sucking ass.

Richard steadied Cass on her feet and then gently let go of her shoulders. Cass spit into the street and wiped the corners of her mouth with her sleeve. Despite the taste in her mouth, she felt better. She felt empty, hollow somehow, cleaned out. But she also felt embarrassed. You didn't see Miranda or Richard doubled over in the street, puking their guts out. Apparently emptying your stomach wasn't standard operating procedure at the end of a vampire fight.

Whatever, Cass thought. *I'm making up my own damn standard procedure for vampire fights.*

Richard put up his hands in surrender, as if Miranda were a cop and she'd just caught him red-handed.

"Step away," Miranda said. "Step. Away."

Richard took a couple steps back.

"That's a good boy."

"Cass, who is this woman?" Richard asked coolly.

"Uhh ... this is my ... aunt?" Cass said, wiping her hands.

She wasn't entirely sure what was happening now. How had Miranda known to come? How did she know Richard? And why was the lightning that shot out of her fingers *green*? A pale blue seemed more Miranda's style.

Cass took a stab at dialing down the tension. She tried making some introductions.

"Miranda, this is my friend, Richard." She paused. "Richard, this is my Aunt Miranda."

It feels a little early for Richard to meet the family, she thought to herself, cringing.

Neither Richard nor Miranda batted an eye at Cass's introductions.

Miranda, for her part, rather than taking the conciliatory hint from Cass, went on the offensive. If anything, the extra time to recover and assess the situation had stoked her anger.

With a wisp of green smoke still curling from her fingertip, she closed the gap between herself and Richard and jabbed him repeatedly in the chest, rattling off a series of questions and accusations.

"How did you find her?" Miranda hissed. "What do you want with her? I know who you are. I know *what* you are."

Richard rocked back on his heels, hands still raised.

"You can't hide from me," she said. Miranda made a gesture like she was enlarging an image on a touch screen and, before Richard knew what was happening,

Miranda issued a command: "In the name of all that is holy, show your true form!"

A window of light opened and framed Richard's playboy face, superimposing a disturbing and ghostly image: it was still clearly Richard, but with fangs, a heavy brow, and pronounced cheekbones.

What the hell? It was the last straw. Cass simply couldn't process what she saw.

Richard, although unperturbed by Miranda's antagonism, snapped when he saw the look of revulsion and confusion cloud Cass's face. "I've worked too hard, come too far, to have things ruined by you, witch!" he snarled, batting Miranda's hands away and breaking the window that they'd framed.

Miranda responded in kind, unleashing some type of force-push that sent Richard stumbling. Richard gathered himself, ready to spring. But before any real damage could be done, Cass jumped between them.

"Stop!" Cass said. "Both of you, stop! I can't deal with this right now. I need you both to calm down. I need you to *talk* to me."

Neither Miranda nor Richard looked inclined to follow these instructions, so Cass pulled out a look borrowed from her mom that she'd been saving for her own kids someday. The look said: *stop right now or you're grounded for a week and won't have dessert for a month.* She leveled the look at both of them in turn and, miraculously, both Miranda and Richard wilted.

"Cass, you can't trust him," Miranda started. "You saw for yourself: he's a vampire. He's not really any different from the dozen or so that already tried to kill you tonight. Don't be fooled."

Richard looked like he didn't know where to start. "Cassandra—" he broke off.

"Well," Cass said, taking his measure and remembering Zach's earlier warning. "Let's have it. Are you? A vampire? Or … whatever?"

Richard looked up and down the street, as if he expected someone to come to his rescue. He licked his lips nervously.

"Cass," he began again, "I'm not what she says. I'm not what you think. Or, at least, not … in the way that she said. I'm not one of the Lost." He took a deep breath. "We can talk about this. But not right now. Not out here. We've got to get off the street. We've got to get out of here."

Cass nodded. They'd been caught up in the moment, but Richard was right. Now that he'd said it, she felt dangerously exposed on the street.

"He's right, Miranda. We can't just stand here and hash this out on the sidewalk."

Miranda reluctantly agreed, but Cass could tell from the look on her face that she was formulating a plan.

"Okay. Toss me your keys, asshole," Miranda said. "I'm driving."

Richard frowned but threw her the keys.

"And you," Miranda continued, pointing at Cass, "you should have known better. Even without my help, you should have known what he was."

Cass didn't understand.

"This piece of work is one thing. But, even more important than him, it's time someone finally told you the truth about *you*."

16

IT WAS LATE. The sun had set but the weather in Spain was beautiful. A warm breeze blew. A sliver of moon shone. The leaves in the trees rustled.

The thin man was waiting, still and silent, in a public park. Three of his "colleagues" accompanied him. He didn't need their help with tonight's job but he did need to manage *their* needs, so he'd brought them along. They were dangerous tools. The three of them fidgeted impatiently, cracking knuckles and shuffling their feet, while he himself stood still, the eye of their gathering storm.

"Shhhh, gentlemen, shhhh," he quieted them.

The four of them were waiting a good ten yards from the path, deep in the shadows, beyond the light cast by the park lights.

As they waited, a pain that felt like a knitting needle jamming into his eye flared in the thin man's head. He made his face into a mask and kept his posture rigid. Showing any weakness in front of his colleagues was a bad idea. He needed to keep an iron grip through this last leg of the journey. He could ride it out it. He'd had a lot of practice. Despite himself, a bead of sweat ran down the side of his pale face. Behind him, he could hear one of his colleagues sniffing the night air. Could they smell his pain? He straightened the cuffs of his suit coat, adjusted the lay of his watch, and dabbed his forehead with a monogrammed handkerchief.

The wind picked up and the trees rustled even more loudly.

If he had still been human, the sound of the trees would have emptied his mind and calmed his heart. But those days were past. His heart no longer beat and his mind did not rest. Instead of his heart, his head throbbed, day and night. The need that drove him pulsed with an unsettling heat.

He touched one finger to his temple and willed the noise to recede—but nothing happened. Whoever's will the incessant throbbing obeyed, it wasn't his. The pain ebbed and flowed through cycles he could never quite predict. And it was getting worse. What used to ache tenderly in quiet moments now imposed itself, regardless of what he was doing, with a sharp bite. It felt, quite literally, like a migraine of the damned.

At the moment, though, the pain was ebbing. It was draining from his head and down into his rotting hand. This was a good sign, at least in the short term. It meant that the tide of pain was going out. Though it made his hand ache, it would be easier for him to work.

The thin man could sense their guest approaching. He would turn the corner soon.

A young priest, out for a late run—trying to exorcise his own demons, no doubt—came into view. The priest was lithe, his shoulders narrow, a runner's body. He flew down the path, gliding effortlessly. The thin man admired his youth and strength.

As the priest closed on their position, the thin man called out in an anxious voice: "Father! Please, help me!"

The priest stopped and peered out into the darkness beyond the path, always ready to help.

"Father!" he called again.

The priest stepped off the path and edged into the dark.

"Hello," he called, "what do you need? How can I help?"

Once the priest had crossed more than half the distance between them, the thin man casually waved his black hand and the bulbs lighting the path burst in a spray of sparks. Then he signaled to his colleagues to circle around and make sure the priest didn't break away.

"Father," he repeated, quietly this time as he approached the priest, "Father, forgive me. But I need your help."

"Who are you? What do you want?" the priest demanded.

This priest thought he was strong. And he thought —mistakenly—that God would protect him.

"Father, your work in the archives is of great interest to me. I understand that you have recently come into possession of some information about the location of a fragment of the One True Cross."

The young priest was nervous now, but still defiant. He shuddered when the speaker materialized, almost ghostly pale, from the deep shadows.

The thin man adjusted his leather gloves.

The priest shook his head, his voice cracking as he said, "I don't know what you're talking about. I can't help you."

His hand went to the small cross around his neck. He snapped its gold chain and held the cross out in front of him, waving it back and forth.

A chorus of angry hisses emerged from the darkness.

The man just laughed his cold laugh.

"Yes, Father, that is what I'm talking about. That is what I'm looking for." He pointed at the cross in his hand. "But I'm not looking for a trinket. I'm looking for the real thing."

As the thin man stepped even closer, the warm breeze failed, the trees fell silent, and a chill crept into the air.

He extended his hand: "Give me the cross, Father."

The priest shook his head again, but his hand trembled.

"There's no need to make this so hard, Father. No need. But you priests always do. It's always the same. If there is one thing that qualifies a man for the priesthood—and I say this having been exposed to an extraordinarily large sample size—it's the uncanny ability to make everything *much* harder than it needs to be. Everything becomes a contest of wills with you priests. Even the most ordinary things get blown up into some kind of cosmic test of your faith. This is not that, Father. No God is watching you. There is only me. And what you hold in your hand cannot save you. It's just a piece of metal. It's just a cheap trinket. All the belief in the world cannot transform it into anything more."

As he gave this little speech, his voice rose and fell with a soothing lilt. But once he'd finished, the command that followed came out almost as a guttural growl: "Now. Hand. It. To. Me."

The priest could barely move. He limply dropped the cross into the man's open palm. In his hand, it melted and then evaporated until no trace of it remained.

The thin man's colleagues almost howled with delight.

"Now that, Father, was a test of good faith. It was a test of your faith—in *me*, the only god you're going to need to worry about tonight. Tell me, then, what I really want to know."

Before the priest could manage a response, the thin man reached out with his now empty hand and seized the priest by his jaw. He lifted him into the air.

"Tell me, Father … tell me…."

Then he reached out with his other hand and pressed his thumb and index finger against the priest's eyes, gradually increasing the pressure.

The priest's body went limp. Then he began speaking, as if in tongues, until an unbroken stream of information about the location of the relic—a verified piece of the true cross itself—poured right out of him.

The thin man nodded appreciatively, noting all of the details he'd need. When the priest lapsed back into strangled silence, he let him drop to the ground.

"Thank you, Father," he whispered.

And then, to his colleagues: "You may have him."

The man turned away from the priest and back toward the darkness of the forest. He felt another wave of black pain gathering strength at the base of his skull.

He ignored the wet sound of tearing flesh and focused on what mattered: soon, he would have gathered enough fragments that a critical mass could be formed. The power of the cross was almost in hand.

17

MIRANDA ALWAYS DROVE fast and recklessly. Today, the problem was compounded by the fact that she didn't normally drive a car that could accelerate from zero to sixty in less than three seconds. And, what's more, she didn't seem to feel the need to adjust her driving style to compensate. As far as Cass could tell—triple-checking her seatbelt as she hung on for dear life in the passenger seat—Miranda's driving only had two settings: an "on" setting where the accelerator was pressed to the floor and an "off" setting where she slammed on the brakes.

From the backseat, as he leaned hard into a sharp turn, his seatbelt cutting into his bruised ribs, Richard politely suggested that Miranda might try the car's self-driving mode.

Miranda's only response was to step harder on the gas.

Richard's face yellowed as they fishtailed again. Cass might have felt sick too if there'd been anything left in her stomach.

Neither Cass nor Richard dared ask where they were going. Miranda seemed to have that part covered. In just a couple of minutes they were out of the city and Miranda took one of the county roads that branched off the interstate. They drove for about twenty miles more until she found what she was looking for. The Model X slalomed into the parking lot of a seedy looking motel and slid to a stop under its broken "No Vacancy" sign. The "No" blinked on and off, sending mixed messages about the availability of a room. Cass took one look at the empty parking lot and the motel's peeling paint and decided they weren't going to have a problem getting a room.

The motel would do. They needed something off the beaten path and they needed a place that would take cash without asking questions.

Miranda banged through the office door and scared the clerk who'd been dozing behind the desk. He gave them a long stare, rubbed his eyes, and looked like he was trying to decide if they were real. Miranda arranged for the room, but when the clerk rang up the charges, Miranda put her hands on her hips, and pointed to Richard: "This asshole's paying."

Richard stepped to the counter, his suit bloody and in tatters. He fished a fat money clip out his pocket and pulled off a hundred dollar bill.

"I can't break that, mister," the clerk objected, waving his hand in the air. "I don't have the change."

Richard pulled an extra hundred off the wad of bills. "Keep the change. And as far anyone knows, we were never here tonight."

The clerk's eyes lit up and a sleazy grin broke across his face as he looked from Richard, to Cass, to Miranda, and then back to Richard. He winked at Richard and then whispered conspiratorially: "I can see that you like them sassy. Your secret's safe with me, mister. Just try not to break the bed or make too much noise."

Miranda groaned, grabbed the key from the counter, and headed for the door.

Richard exchanged an innocent look with Cass and shrugged his shoulders.

"Right," Cass offered, rolling her eyes, "this kind of thing must happen to you all the time."

The room was a disaster. Cass couldn't imagine any circumstances in which she'd be willing to get into that bed. She could almost hear the bed bugs salivating. But it didn't matter. They weren't spending the night. They just needed a chance to catch their breath, clean up, and talk.

Richard and Cass were both a bit worse for the wear but Richard was in the worst shape by far. He slipped off his suit coat and tossed it into the trash. He peeled off what was left of his shirt and, wincing, tried to use the mirror to get a look at the cuts and bruises on his back. He couldn't find an angle that worked.

Miranda stepped outside to make a call.

"Let me help," Cass said.

Richard grunted and leaned against the sink, rolling his broad shoulders.

Cass wetted a towel and wiped away the blood. She gently poked a cut or two, gauging their depth. The bruises would hurt for days, but the cuts all seemed superficial. She was more shocked to see that his back was already covered in scars—very old, very deep scars —that weren't immediately obvious from across the room. He looked like he'd been whipped. Without quite meaning to, she lightly traced the line of one especially long scar with the tip of her finger as it arced diagonally down his shoulder and across his spine.

Richard shivered.

"Thank you, Cassandra," he said abruptly, obviously embarrassed. He grabbed his travel bag from the bed and closed the bathroom door behind him. Steam from the shower curled out from under the door.

Get a grip Jones. What do you think this is? An episode of The Bachelorette?

Richard returned in a couple of minutes wearing slim blue jeans and a white button-down shirt. Both looked like they cost more than her weekly salary.

Miranda returned after Cass had showered and changed. She'd come back with a pile of snacks and sodas raided from the vending machines and stacked them in the center of the room's small table. They gathered all around and sat down to talk. Miranda sat on one side, Richard on the other, with Cass positioned in the middle.

Cass was sure this little summit would quickly devolve into name-calling if she didn't take the reins. With pen and pad in hand and her hair pulled back, she put on a confident, scholarly look. Part of her wished she had glasses to nail the part and part of her thought this whole train of thought was bullshit.

I am a damn scholar! That's why the whole world is chasing me in the first place! Time to inject a little rationality into ... whatever the hell this is.

"You," she pointed at Miranda, "you're first."

Miranda sat up a little straighter.

"You can shoot green lightning out of your fingertips?"

"Yes," Miranda admitted. "Sometimes."

"Why?"

"Ok, I know you need answers, but for right now the simplest explanation is ..." Miranda paused, an uncharacteristic look of uncertainty flashing across her face.

"Magic?"

"Yes. That'll work. For now."

"And vampires are real?"

Miranda shot a look at Richard. "Indeed," she said.

Cass rubbed her pendant. She knew exactly what she wanted to ask next—*Did my mother know about all this?*—but she was also pretty sure she wasn't ready to hear the answer.

"And you," Cass swiveled to face Richard, "you are a vampire?"

Richard hesitated but when Miranda looked ready to answer for him, he relented. "Yes."

Cass felt her weak eye focus and clear.

Goddamn. They're telling the truth.

Seeing her surprise, he went on. "I still breathe. I still sleep. If hurt, I bleed. I'm still very human, I've just been around for … for a long time."

Miranda huffed, and after an irate glance Richard continued. "So I am, technically, a vampire. But I'm not what she says." He stood up and paced to the bathroom door and back, rubbing the stubble on his chin. He sat back down. "I'm not like … *them*. I'm not like the ones who came after you tonight. It's true that I'm not quite human anymore. I haven't been for a long time. But I'm not quite a vampire either." He paused, weighing his words. "I'm Turned, but I'm not … *Lost*."

Miranda sneered at this but, again, Richard's words rang true to Cass.

Now it was Miranda's turn to pace. She stood up, went to the window, crossed her arms, and surveyed the parking lot through a crack in the curtains. Rain occasionally pattered lightly against the glass. It was a little too easy for Cass to imagine the trees out there filled with more vampires, hanging upside down like huge bats, just waiting for the right moment to strike. She shook the thought from her head.

They *would* need to wrap this up soon, and move on.

"What's the difference" Cass asked, "between Turned and Lost? And is it a difference that matters?"

Miranda jumped in. "The only difference, Cass, is that he hasn't eaten anyone—*yet*."

"In part," Richard responded, reaching out to squeeze Cass's hand. "But the differences are crucial. Only the Lost need to feed on human blood, are hurt by sunlight, fail to cast a reflection, et cetera. Only the Lost have abandoned their humanity. Only the Lost are beyond redemption. The rest of us persist, but out of our times. Animal blood is enough for us. And we—like every human being—must wake up every day and decide again whether we will use what life is left to us for good or ill."

Miranda seemed to grudgingly grant the point.

Cass turned this over in her mind. She peeled the wrapper off a Snickers bar and ate the whole thing in three bites. She popped open a can of Coke Zero, drank half, burped, and drank the rest.

She looked at the two of them watching her.

"What?"

"Feeling better?" Miranda asked.

Cass sucked a smear of chocolate off her thumb and took her pen and pad back in hand. She knew what had to be asked next and frowned.

"And what about me, Miranda? What exactly am I?"

Miranda turned from the window and sat back in her chair. She gently lifted Cass's chin and turned her face toward her own. She touched the corner of Cass's eye with the tip of her finger.

"You," Miranda said, "are what you were born to be. You are your mother's daughter. You have the power to see through the lies that cloud our world and cut to the heart of truth. Sometimes this power shows itself in your interactions with other people. Sometimes in your ability to sift information as a scholar. Sometimes in your skill as a fighter."

Richard perked up at this, a look of recognition dawning across his face, as if several pieces of a puzzle had just snapped together for him.

"Of course," Richard said, almost to himself. "Of course. Why didn't I see it? You, Cassandra, are a *Seer*."

Miranda didn't object.

"Finding you was no accident," Richard continued. "If the race to find the One True Cross with your help was urgent before, it's doubly so now. You, Cassandra Jones, are the key a thousand-year-old mystery. And you can't be replaced."

18

"IF ALL THIS is true," Cass said, "then it's time to go. It's time to get out of the city and get to work. None of what I've learned tonight changes what I already promised to do. It doesn't change any of the decisions I've already made."

Cass stood up and grabbed her bag off the bed. She stuffed her pad, pen, and a couple of other loose items back into it and then surveyed the room for anything she might have forgotten.

Richard and Miranda were still sitting at the table. They looked at each other and then back to Cass.

"What are you waiting for? We're going to the airfield," Cass snapped.

"The airfield?" Miranda asked.

Cass turned to Richard. "Our private jet is still waiting for us, Mr. Bigshot?"

"Yes, of course," Richard confirmed.

"Then let's go," Cass said, scooping the remaining candy off the table and into her bag. She zipped the bag closed, thought for a moment, unzipped it, fished out a Kit-Kat, and then zipped it closed again. Holding the Kit-Kat between her teeth, she laced up her worn leather hiking boots and slipped into her puffy down jacket. She flipped up the hood and tore the corner off the candy bar wrapper. She patted the hard rectangle of her phone in the pocket of her jeans and thought about Zach but decided again that he would have to wait for later.

Richard and Miranda were still frozen at the table.

Cass clapped her hands. "I said, let's go, people!"

As if a spell had been broken, they both jumped up and gathered their stuff.

When Richard pulled on his leather jacket, Cass almost laughed out loud.

Ha! I knew it! They do have a damn dress code!

Richard caught her smiling at him and smiled back.

They loaded up the car. Miranda insisted on driving again. Both Cass and Richard blanched, but Miranda still had the keys and no one was going to fight her for them.

"We'll go the airport," Miranda said, "but we have to make one more stop before do, even if it's a little risky. And that's non-negotiable."

Both the airport and their stop were on the far side of the city. Miranda's driving settled into something approaching normalcy and the heat from the vents, combined with the hypnotic swish of the windshield wipers, forced Cass to recognize how tired she really was.

Richard had nodded off in the backseat and Cass was almost gone herself when Miranda squeezed Cass's knee. Cass jerked back awake but calmed when Miranda reassuringly shushed her.

"I'm sorry, Cass," Miranda started, keeping her voice low. "I'm sorry that I didn't say more, sooner. But your dad … when your mom died, your dad didn't want you to have anything to do with me."

Cass just waited and listened, eyes focused on the black road ahead. She was wide awake now.

"He wanted to protect you. He wanted to close the two of you up in a protective shell made of books and green tea. And part of me wanted the same. And so I let him and I tried to stay out of the way."

Cass nodded. This was true. And, mostly, it had worked. She and her dad had lived inside of that shell of books ever since her mom had died. And, until recently, they'd been living there together. They couldn't have stayed there forever, but she was glad her dad had made it last as long as he had.

"Your mom was just about to start training you when she died. In some ways, she had already started."

Cass thought about all the games they'd used to play, games her mom had made up. And she thought about how, almost as soon as she'd been old enough to walk, her mom had wanted her to be able to stand up for herself, to defend herself and fight for herself. When she was just three, her mom had enrolled her in her first martial arts class. Cass had a rainbow of belts and a collection of tournament trophies in her old room.

Once her mom was gone, Cass had channeled of lot of her anger and grief into honing those very skills her mother had wanted her to have. Her lean body and lethal skills were, in many ways, a living monument to her mother's memory.

"But your dad was reluctant, and your mom waited … and then it was too late."

Cass turned her face toward her door and wiped the corner of her eye.

"I don't have time to explain this all now. Your mother was powerful and well-known in the world of magic. But the one thing you *must* understand about your own powers is that they have a clearly defined limit. As a Seer you have the power to *see* the truth, but this power to see the truth depends on you're *being* truthful. Lying, even to yourself, will weaken that power."

Cass thought immediately of what had happened earlier tonight when, she had lied about trusting Richard and her power had faltered, putting them both at risk.

Note to self, Cass thought, *brutal honesty is no longer optional.*

Cass nodded and squeezed Miranda's hand.

"Thank you, Miranda," Cass whispered. "Thank you for being there tonight. And thank you for being here now."

"Oh, girl," Miranda cooed, "I will always be there for you."

The sun would be up in another hour, but for now the streets were still dark. Cass had been so absorbed by her memories and her conversation with Miranda that she hadn't realized where they were going until they'd almost pulled into the driveway.

When they got to the door and rang the doorbell, she knew they didn't need to worry about disturbing anyone. She knew he'd already be awake.

A balding man with soft edges and a sweater answered the door. His Japanese ancestry was obvious.

Before he could take in the scene and register Miranda's presence, Cass took the lead. She wanted to make the first impression. She hadn't known for sure how she'd feel when he opened the door but, once he had, her response was spontaneous. She rushed into his arms, hugged him tight, and buried her head in his shoulder.

"Hi, dad," she whispered in his ear. "I'm home."

19

GARY JONES RETURNED her fierce hug. Although he'd seemed surprised to see her, he was obviously glad she was there. He went stiff, though, when he saw both Miranda and Richard hanging back. He immediately assumed the worst—and he wasn't far off. Cass really had had a pretty harrowing night.

"Are you okay, Cass? Are you hurt?"

He held her out at arm's length, trying to get a good look at her on the dark doorstep.

Cass held up her hands and turned them front and back as if to say: look Dad, I'm fine! But even the dim light from inside the house was enough to show the bruise spreading across her cheek. Cass let her hair fall to curtain that side of her face but it was too little, too late.

The same dark expression that had crossed Zach's face when he'd seen the bruise now crossed her father's. He transformed from mild mannered librarian to protective father in an instant. But, rather than aiming his anger at Richard, he was already primed to go after Miranda.

What am I, a porcelain doll?

Cass was getting tired of the men who cared about her reacting that way.

I'm the one with a car trunk full of swords!

It was easy to see that Miranda's first instinct was to fight fire with fire. But when she saw the pleading look in Cass's eyes, she held off.

"I told you to stay away from her," Gary said through clenched teeth. "I asked you to stay away. I knew this would happen. I knew where this would lead." He stepped off the porch, closing the gap between himself and Miranda.

Cass tried to redirect his attention.

"Dad, wait!" she said, touching him on his shoulder. "Dad, it's not what you think."

But he couldn't hear her. The angry words came pouring out him, like he'd had them bottled and ready to go for years, just waiting for the right moment.

"It always the same thing with you, Miranda. It always ends the same way. You're big on *adventure*, but the roads you travel all lead to the same place. You're playing with powers you don't understand and can't control. And who suffers, Miranda? Who?" His voice rose until he was shouting.

Shit, Cass thought, *dad's gone nuclear.*

Again, it looked for an instant like Miranda would respond in kind, launching her own salvo of missiles. But she didn't. She stepped back and let herself absorb the force of what Gary had said, acknowledging some of the truth in it.

"Who? Who suffers, Gary?" Miranda echoed. "You do. Rose did. I do. Cass has and will."

Silence. Even the birds stopped singing their early morning song. No one moved.

The look on Cass's father's face changed from anger to confusion. He hadn't expected her to agree.

"I'm sorry, Gary. I'm so sorry," Miranda continued. "But some things are bigger than us. And where this goes now isn't up to us. And it sure as hell is no longer just *about* us. You've tried hard to keep Cass safe and you've done a good job. But Cass can only ignore what she is for so long. Eventually the cost of pretending to be something she isn't will, all by itself, destroy her."

Gary's face had softened, like he had almost been ready to accept Miranda's unexpected apology. But when Miranda didn't stop there, when she circled back around to Cass again, he wasn't in a place where he could hear what she was saying. His eyes hardened and his jaw clenched again.

"No," was all he could manage, shaking his head. "No."

He turned back to Cass.

"Dad, this isn't Miranda's fault. She's not responsible for the trouble we're in. She did stay away—mostly. And if she hadn't shown up tonight, Richard and I would be dead."

Cass pulled him back into a hug.

"She saved us, Dad. She *saved* us."

Her father didn't need any special powers to feel the force of this and to have it temper his fear and anger. He squeezed Cass tight, like he had when she was little, and only gradually let her go.

He looked at Richard, obviously not pleased by his playboy vibe, and then at Miranda. He paused for a moment as their eyes met and a beat passed between them with the force of a grudging thank-you. But rather than saying anything out loud, he settled for ushering their little group into the house.

"Come, come into the house," he said. "It's ridiculous to stand out here at this hour. Leave your shoes by the door."

This invitation clearly didn't mean that all was forgiven. But it did, at least, signal a truce.

They all filed through the door behind him and gathered in the kitchen. Cass got some coffee brewing. Then, around the kitchen table, Cass recounted the events of the last couple of days. She tried not to leave anything out, even the crazy stuff. She expected her dad to balk at the stuff about vampires—he did cock an eyebrow and shift uncomfortably in his seat, gauging the distance to the butcher's block full of knives on the counter, when she revealed that Richard was a vampire —or at the stuff about her own powers. But he didn't. He swallowed the whole story as if he'd known about such things all along and had been expecting to hear about it from her for years. Maybe he had.

What do *you know, Dad?* Cass wondered. *How much do you know? Who are you under all those books?*

Once Cass had finished, the conversation quickly funneled down to the only real question at hand: where, exactly, was their private jet headed in search of the One True Cross?

"Our best lead at the moment is Valencia, Spain," Richard offered. "I think we'll start there."

"Yes, interesting," Gary said, scratching his chin and pulling off his glasses to rub them clean with his shirt. "Saint Peter is reported to have traveled through Valencia. And, obviously, it is already the resting place of a famous relic, the Holy Chalice. Some believe that this chalice is the very cup used by Christ at the Last Supper."

"Right," Cass said, "and I'm Mother Teresa." She held up the sugar shaker. "This sugar shaker is as likely to be the real chalice. Even if we ignore the the competing claims from other chalices, the material and craftsmanship of that relic in Valencia don't fit the bill at all."

Gary took the shaker from her and add a little extra to his coffee. He stirred the sugar in, making that thoughtful sound that comes from a metal spoon lightly scraping against the sides of a ceramic cup.

"Wait a moment," he said. He got up from the table and went back to his office. They could hear him rooting around in his papers. He came back with a sheaf of loose notes and photocopied manuscript pages.

"Valencia might not be a bad place to start. Cass is right that the Holy Chalice is a dead end, you won't find any clues there. But there *is* a small town north of Valencia named Meliana with a small but extraordinarily old chapel that has, for years, been rumored to be associated with the One True Cross."

Cass pulled out her laptop. Her dad had triggered a memory. Meliana sounded familiar. She clicked and swiped until she found what she was looking for.

"Yes," she said, tapping her screen. "This is the place to start. A host of independent lines of evidence all intersect outside of Valencia. And if I take into account the new information Richard shared with me earlier tonight, it looks decisive. That old chapel in Meliana is ground zero."

Cass's eyes were bright. This is what she loved most of all.

Screw the swordplay, give me a library any day.

"Yes," her father agreed. "I think you've got something here."

Cass flushed with pleasure at her father's agreement. She leaned back in her chair, ran her fingers through her hair, and absently pulled at her pendant.

Gary had started to say something else but, when his voice trailed off, Cass saw that he was staring at her necklace. He reached out to touch it.

"You still wear this?" he asked. "It was your mother's. She wore it for years." His eyes grew distant. "She was wearing it the first time we met."

Everyone waited, silent, until Gary shook himself and rejoined them in the present.

When he did, he looked straight at Miranda: "Go. Go do what you must."

Then, the fire returning to his voice, "But if you let anything happen to Cass, you'll find that I have powers of my own that I won't be able to control."

20

WHILE RICHARD MADE arrangements with his pilot and Miranda talked privately with Gary, Cass retreated to her old bedroom on the first floor.

She hadn't lived there since her senior year in high school, but the room still looked exactly the same: heavy dark curtains, piles of books everywhere, trophies on shelves, cheap swords on the wall, and a closet full of goth clothes she'd tried out her senior year but abandoned as too much effort when she'd started her freshman year at Stanford.

She collapsed onto her bed and curled up with an old pillow, trying not to think about anything in particular. She took a look around the room.

So dark, she thought. *What was I thinking? Even the curtains are black!*

Had she been destined to get involved with vampires all along? Was her room evidence of this? Was Richard going to make her drag out her black leather jacket, draped with silver chains, and then buckle on the leather choker with studs that she was pretty sure was still in her jewelry box? If he asked her, would she want to?

She tried imagining Richard with some smoky eye shadow and the leather choker. Then, inevitably, she imagined him wearing *just* the eye shadow and leather choker.

Not helpful, Jones. Not. Helpful.

Shaking her head free of that thought, her limbic system defiantly tried substituting an image of Zach in eye shadow and choker—*Zach! Shit!*—but a wave of guilt shut that down before it had a chance to go anywhere. She'd promised to text to him if anything else happened. A lot *had* happened and she hadn't called or texted him.

She'd better check in with him. She rolled over and pulled out her phone. She tried to figure out what to say.

Almost eaten by 12 more vamps. Richard a vamp, but not the bad kind. Aunt is a witch. Dad melting down. On the lam. Headed to Spain. How was your night?

That probably wasn't the best approach to take.

She settled for a ping: *You there?*

She thought he might still be asleep, so she didn't expect an immediate answer. But before she could put down her phone, it buzzed.

Open your window, it said.

What the hell? What kind of advice is that? Cass wondered. *Does he think I need some fresh air?*

She tried a snarky response: *No, open YOUR window.*

Can't, came the response.

Why?

Too far away.

What? Where are you?

Outside.

Outside where?

Your window.

Cass pulled back her curtain and almost fell off her bed: Zach's crooked grin was pressed up against the glass.

What the hell?

She popped open her window but before she could say anything, Zach shushed her.

"Are you okay?" he whispered.

"What? Yes, I'm fine," she said in her normal voice.

"Shhhhh."

"What? Why are we whispering," Cass stage-whispered.

Zach started to climb through the window, the wooden stake in his right hand complicating the maneuver.

"Is he holding you hostage? Is your dad okay? What room is he in?" Zach whispered urgently.

Cass thought for a second that he was kidding. Then she registered the earnest look on his face and the wooden stake in his hand and couldn't keep herself from laughing out loud.

It started with just a giggle, but after a night full of absurdities, this one was too much. Zach tried to shush her again, still deadly earnest, but this just pushed her over the edge. She sat down hard on the floor and laughed so hard tears streamed down her face. It was a great relief. Cass could feel all the tension she'd been holding inside—like she'd been holding her breath for hours—escape all at once with a pleasant whoosh.

Zach looked surprised by her reaction, then confused, and then a bit hurt. "Hey!" he whispered fiercely, "I'm trying to rescue you here! Why are you laughing?"

But before his face could turn too red, Cass, from her knees, pulled him into a hug.

"Thank you," she said, "thank you, Zach for … saving me." And she meant it. But before she could get the whole sentence out, she started laughing again, hanging from Zach's neck. Before long her infectious laughter got Zach going too and they both fell back onto the floor into a heap of arms and legs.

At just that moment, Gary burst into the room with Richard right on his heels, both of them expecting trouble.

Cass tried to pull herself together and wave them off, stifling the old feeling that her dad just caught her alone in her room with a boy.

"We're fine, we're fine—" she said.

Her father raised an eyebrow, as if to ask about the identity of this mystery guest who'd climbed in through the window of her bedroom. Cass attempted to oblige through fits of giggles.

"Dad, this is my friend Zach. Zach, my dad," she finally managed.

Zach tried to explain why he was there. When he hadn't heard anything from Cass, he'd gone back to her apartment. And when he saw the wreckage they'd left behind in the street, he feared the worst. He hadn't been to her dad's house before but it wasn't hard to find and it was really the only place he could think to look beside the coffeehouse. Seeing Richard's car in the driveway, he thought he'd better circle the house and see if he could tell what was happening inside. When Cass sent her text, he'd just been crawling through the bushes outside her window.

This story may have been the least weird part of the last twenty-four hours. Nobody thought twice about it. Once Zach had said his piece, they explained their own plan to Zach.

His response was immediate.

"I'm coming with you," Zach said.

Richard and Miranda immediately began to protest, but as soon as he'd said it, Cass's eye twitched and focused. It *felt* right. And it felt *good* to have Zach here. Whatever they'd be facing next, her gut told her that she would need his help.

"Quiet," Cass interjected. "Zach's right. He's coming with us. This isn't up for a vote."

Zach shot her a grateful look.

"We need him," she said. "You've already got your team of people, Richard. Zach and Miranda are mine. We all go together or we don't go at all."

Leaving the country unannounced for who knows how long could mean the abrupt end of her and Zach's shared dream to be baristas for the rest of their lives, but Cass was willing to risk it.

"Fine," Richard reluctantly agreed, eyeing Zach distrustfully. "But it's time to go. Our ride is ready and waiting."

It only took a few minutes to gather their things and pack the car. Cass pulled an extra black t-shirt out of her closet and threw it in her bag—but left the leather jacket and the choker.

Richard, Miranda, and Zach piled into the car.

Miranda still had the keys.

Cass hesitated at the door, unsure how to say good-bye to her dad, unsure about when—or even if—she'd see him again. She sensed the same hesitation in him. But this was too important a moment to shrug off.

She stopped wavering and hugged him. He squeezed her back.

"I'm sorry, Dad," she said. "I know this isn't what you wanted for me. I love you. And I'll be back. I promise."

She expected him to say something in return but he didn't. Or couldn't. He squeezed her tighter and then just said, "Wait here." He disappeared back into the house.

He returned in a minute, holding a long leather box with an ornate handle and clasp. It looked very old and very valuable.

"I see," he began, his eyes wet, "that you still wear your mother's necklace. And I'm glad. You are so much like your mother."

He stopped for a moment and swallowed hard. Cass didn't try to rush him.

"This," he said, "was also your mother's. Though, given what lies ahead, I suspect that it may be more immediately useful to you. She, I know, intended you to have it."

With that, he opened the case and revealed an ancient katana, clearly priceless.

Cass lifted it from the box and tested its weight and balance. It was phenomenally light and strong. She took a practice stroke or two and the blade sang as it sliced through the air. The edge was supernaturally sharp.

Cass sheathed the sword and bowed to her father.

He carefully closed the case, bowed in turn, and, without another word from either of them, went back into the house and shut the door.

21

MIRANDA AND CASS sat in front. Richard and Zach were in back.

Having already been through the wringer twice, Cass and Richard steeled themselves for more of Miranda's driving. Cass scooted her seat up a little, braced her feet, and made sure she had a good grip on her door. Richard wedged himself into the corner of his seat. But Zach had no idea what he was getting into. He hadn't even fastened his seatbelt when Miranda fishtailed out of the Jones's driveway in a cloud of smoke and rubber.

Richard chuckled under his breath as he watched Zach struggle and fail for several blocks to just get his seatbelt fastened. Zach's face was getting red, but there wasn't much he could do. He couldn't complain about Cass's aunt. His personal code of chivalry wouldn't allow it. Cass heard Zach start to say something and then bite his tongue a couple of times. And he definitely couldn't complain about the car itself. Complaining about the car would be the same thing as acknowledging how amazing the car was—and there was no way he was going to give Richard that pleasure.

So when they slammed around another corner at thirty miles an hour and Zach ended up in Richard's lap for the third time in five minutes, he had no one to get angry at but Richard.

Cass could feel the tension growing in the backseat. She knew that Zach and Richard had distrusted each other from the start, but she also knew—and couldn't help but enjoy—that some of this tension was about her.

She'd had good friends, and even a couple of boyfriends, over the years, but nothing serious. And her poor people skills, wobbly eye, walled off emotions, love of martial arts, and tendency to choose books over people meant that she'd never been the focal point of a love triangle. Clearly this wasn't quite that, but it felt close enough to be flattering.

She pulled down her visor and flipped open the mirror. She pulled her hair back into a ponytail but also snuck a look into the backseat. Richard and Zach were a pretty stark contrast. Jet-set hedge fund manager versus local barista. Ivy league versus community college. English versus Latino. Suit versus jeans. Luxury car versus moped. Slick versus funny. Vampire versus … not a vampire.

The differences ran deep. And they were more than cosmetic. Richard clearly knew what he was talking about when it came to the historical and archeological details of their search but Cass couldn't in a million years picture him cleaning the toilets at Java's Palace.

Still, maybe these differences were why she felt like she was going to need them both. Maybe these differences were part of why her gut insisted that she bring Zach.

While she was running through this whole thread in her mind, Cass had zoned out and Richard caught her staring at him in the mirror. He smiled and winked. Cass, embarrassed, flipped up her visor and tried to stare out the window. But Zach had seen the smile and wink and it was just salt in his wound.

Richard, a little too pleased with himself, wasn't paying close attention when they took the next corner and this time it was his turn to lose his balance and end up in Zach's lap.

"Sit. Up. Asshole," Zach grunted. "Get off me."

Zach's accompanying shove was a bit too strong and Richard ended up bumping his head against his door.

"Watch it, wanker," Richard said, rubbing the bruise.

Miranda floored the accelerator again and pressed the whole lot of them deep into their seats.

"Cass," Richard started, "do we *really* need to bring"— He waved his thumb in Zach's direction— "him? I've got a whole damn team of professionals waiting to help us."

Zach looked worried for a moment. But Cass didn't hesitate to reaffirm her position: "We need him. He's coming. That's all there is to it."

Zach, emboldened by Cass's support, couldn't resist a little snark of his own. "Cass, do we *really* need the international man of mystery, here? As a general rule, shouldn't we try to limit the number of vampires on any given expedition to, I don't know, say: *zero*?"

As Zach was saying this, Miranda sped through the gate and onto the private airstrip they'd been aiming for. She slammed on the brakes and then skidded to a stop near the private jet that was already fueled and waiting for them on the small runway.

The jet had "The York Group" stenciled in bold red letters on its side.

Richard looked at Cass, then out the window at the jet, and then back at Zach. He gave Zach a big shit-eating grin.

"Let's take my plane," Richard said. "Unless, of course, you'd prefer, Zach, to take yours?"

Cass and Miranda rolled their eyes.

"Put away the rulers and zip up your pants, boys," Miranda sniped. "We've got a flight to catch."

22

THE THIN MAN and his colleagues would need to finish quickly and leave before daybreak. They couldn't afford to be caught in the sun or get trapped inside for the duration of the day.

The thin man's face was free of worry. He'd calculated how much time this would take and he knew exactly what time the sun would rise.

His two colleagues, however, were not as precise nor meticulous. They tended to be anxious and high strung —their capacity for reason always seemed to get compromised by their transformation and the blinding hunger that came with it—and their trust in him, while firm, only went so far. It seemed to him that each new generation was worse than the last, weaker and hungrier and dumber, more prone to be overwhelmed by their passions and emotions, more likely to turn feral.

Still, even if his calculations were spot on, they'd better hurry.

Things had already taken too long with this last priest. The older these priests got, they more stubborn they became, as if faith were a bad habit they couldn't kick. This old man had been much worse than the young one in the park. In the end, they hadn't been able to bend him to their purposes. He'd simply broken rather than yield. What a mess. Regrettable. They had had no choice but to swap in a crude understudy to play the part of the "helpful priest" instead.

It would be worth it, though.

Now that he'd set Cassandra Jones in motion, he needed to steer her in directions that would be useful to him. He'd recently received reports that, even now, she and Richard York were in the air, winging their way to Spain. But, like a game of chess, he was several moves ahead. She would help him whether she intended to or not.

The thin man planted his present for the priest to offer Cassandra and brushed the dust from the sleeves of his suit.

"You, bring the car around," the thin man ordered, pointing to one of this colleagues. "And be quick.

"And you," he said, pointing to the other, "make sure we've left no trace."

Checking the sleeves of his suit one last time, he exited through the rear of the house and cut through the chapel. Sunlight was already streaming through an upper window on the eastern wall. Sticking to the shadows, he slipped out a side exit and into the backseat of his waiting Mercedes—black paint, darkly tinted windows.

He flexed his gloved fingers, absorbed the pain, and straightened his already straight tie. The black skin and dead flesh had spread almost to his shoulder. Time, in general, was growing very short. He could deal with the pain—for now. But he didn't want to know what would happen when it reached his heart.

"Drive," he said.

23

IT WAS LATE afternoon by the time they touched down in Spain.

Zach had snored the whole way. Miranda had nibbled automatically at the snacks, mostly staring out her window, silent, gathering her strength. Richard had spent the whole trip on the phone managing a billion-dollar hedge fund and consulting with his team of archeologists, historians, and scientists. Cass had slept a little but used most of the flight to review her notes, sorting through what material she already had about Meliana. She found some details about the old chapel but she was especially pleased to rediscover a note that, about a year ago, she'd spoken to an old priest attached to that chapel as part of her research. Their conversation had been brief and her notes were sparse, but that prior connection could be enough to open the door for them.

They were winding, now, through a nest of narrow streets in Meliana in a rental BMW. Richard had kept a firm grip on the keys. Everyone—except Miranda—was grateful that he was driving. Miranda had claimed shotgun, though, and as they drove through the town, she constantly tapped her right foot on the car's floor, as if she could make Richard drive faster by pressing on her own imaginary gas pedal.

Could she? Cass wondered, watching Miranda stomp again when a small opening presented itself in traffic. *Could Miranda actually make the car go faster with her imaginary gas pedal? What* can *witches do, anyway? Does magic have its own set of rules? Are cars fair game? Could Miranda supercharge the engine with green lightning?*

Cass and Zach had the backseat.

Cass rapped her knuckle absently against her window, watching people pass on the street.

Her bag and her mother's sword were stuffed into the backseat with her. She gripped the leather hilt. It couldn't have fit better in her hand. It felt almost alive in response to her touch.

She splayed her fingers and took a closer look at her hand. Of course the grip fit. Now that she dared think about it for the first time in years, it was obvious to her that her hand *was* her mother's hand. Her fingers were long and true, the nails were short and practical, the wrist was strong. She hadn't seen her mother's hand in more than a decade, but she would recognize it immediately. And she would never forget what it felt like to hold that hand.

Zach watched her turn over her own hand, examining it, and smiled. He gave her a wink.

If Zach held her hand, Cass wondered, would he be able to feel what it had felt like to hold her mother's? Cass winked back. She let her hand fall and rest again on the sword's hilt.

Her thoughts were drifting again when Richard stomped on the brakes and Miranda yelled, "Watch out!" Cass's seatbelt bit into her shoulder and, as the car jerked to a stop, she caught just a glimpse of an orange tabby streak into the nearest alley. The cat reminded her of Atlantis. *Are orange tabby cats common in Spain?* Who knew.

Richard and Miranda argued for a moment about his driving, until Richard got them underway again.

"Do you need me to drive, pretty boy?" Miranda asked gruffly, a green glint in her eye.

The glint was playful but it still sent a shiver down Cass's spine. Even such a small reminder of Miranda's powers scared her a little, mostly, she suspected, because if Miranda's powers were, in fact, batshit crazy, then what did that say about Cass's own? Cass had to admit that weird stuff wasn't just happening *to* her. A lot of the weird stuff going on *was* her. This was both thrilling and terrifying.

Who the hell am I? She asked herself. *Or, better, what the hell am I?*

She didn't know how to frame the question, let alone answer it. She gripped the sword's pommel more tightly.

Just hang in there, Jones. Hang on tight. Trust yourself. Trust the people you're with. And for Christ's sake: don't forget to tell the truth.

This was a good reminder. She should probably get it tattooed on her forearm—"Tell. The. Truth."—in big block letters, stretching from her elbow to her wrist. To be honest, the less she was going to need her powers, the better. But if push came to shove, she wanted to be able to call on them.

As the Spanish city streaked by, Cass closed her eyes and tried to feel around inside her own head. Could she tap into her powers, right now, at will? She wasn't sure what to do or what to look for. She tried thinking the words: *Power on!* But she just felt ridiculous and nothing happened. She thought that maybe she had to say something out loud, but she couldn't do that now, in the backseat. Plus, she was pretty sure that "Power on!" was not the magic phrase.

Cass took a deep breath, settled back into her seat, and tried to let her breathing sweep her mind free of distraction. But the emptier her mind became and the further away her emotions felt, the less powerful she felt. Then, just as she was about to give up, she felt her weak eye twitch. And deep behind the eye, deep in the heart of that emptiness, she felt a hint of warmth.

Bingo, she thought. *Of course.*

She centered her attention on the hint of warmth and when she did, she could feel her vision clearing a little and everything seemed to slow just a bit. She felt a kind of … *readiness* creep into her bones.

She opened her eyes and looked out the window. A woman and child passed by, hand in hand, in slow motion. She felt like she could read them almost without effort, as if the truth about them had risen from deep inside of them to the surface, visible now to everyone. The woman was frustrated, the child was angry. This woman was not the child's birth mother.

She saw a middle-aged man walk quickly the other way. He presented as a mix of shame and satisfaction, returning home from an afternoon with his mistress.

She turned to look out Zach's window but saw, instead, Zach looking right back at her, with a curious expression on his face.

She immediately saw the truth of him, plain as day, like a door had opened for her into his mind: he loved her.

She didn't know what to do with this—did she want him to love her?—and then felt ashamed of herself, as if she'd just been caught looking through a stranger's underwear drawer. Her attention broke and she blushed furiously.

Zach raised a finger and gestured toward her eye. "Cass," he started, "what's going on with your eye? It's … not like it normally is."

But even as he said this, with her attention broken, her eye clouded and shifted out of focus. The thread had broken.

"Oh," Zach said, watching her eye, confused, "never mind. It must have just been the light."

And then Zach, too, just looked like normal Zach.

"We're here," Richard said. Unnoticed by Zach and Cass, he'd already stopped the car in front of the old chapel and had turned to look at them.

When neither Zach nor Cass moved to get out, Richard tried again: "Hello? Anyone home? We're here."

Cass pulled herself together.

"Right, let's go." She said. "Richard, you stay here. Keep the car ready in case we have to leave in a rush. Zach and Miranda, with me."

Cass popped the car door, but hesitated for a moment before exiting.

Should I bring the sword? Her hand itched to hold it. *Probably not the best ice breaker, Jones. Let's pretend you're a normal human being and try talking first. Then, later, you can dice things up if you need to.*

Miranda and Zach hung back. Cass approached and knocked on the door of the small residence adjoined to the chapel. She tried to retrieve some of the focus she'd lost just a minute ago.

A very old, very sick looking man in a priest's collar opened the door.

"Yes?" he asked. "Who are you? What do you want?"

24

Cass looked Father Vizzini up and down. His clothes were worn and ill-fitting, his hair wild, his face un-shaved. He pulled uncomfortably at his clerical collar with one finger like he'd never worn one before. He wasn't what she'd expected. But, then again, Cass had met enough priests to know that, outside of a cathedral, they were rarely what people expected. Priests were people, too.

He looked a little unsteady on his feet and Cass had to resist the temptation to reach out and prop him up. She glanced over her shoulder, checking to see what Zach and Miranda thought. Miranda looked skeptical. Zach just winked, smiled his crooked smile, and shrugged. Five minutes ago that wink would have just made her roll her eyes but now it seemed to mean something more.

Could Zach tell something was different? Did he know that she knew? Or, perhaps even more to the point, did *she* know what she thought she knew? Did she know *anything*? Could she trust her powers?

Focus, Jones!

She turned her attention back to Vizzini, held out her hand, and introduced herself. He looked at her hand nervously for a moment but took it. Then, before she'd had a chance to offer any real explanation of why they were there, he was already inviting them, as if he'd been expecting them. Cass found this odd, but brushed it off.

They crowded into the sitting room of the small house and the three of them all squeezed, hip to hip, onto a tiny, low slung sofa. With her knees higher than eye-level, Cass felt like a giant doll sitting on a toy couch. Zach looked even more ridiculous. She doubted he was going to be able to stand back up. Vizzini took an old rocking chair opposite them and immediately started rocking back and forth, creaking loudly with every pass.

"What can I help you with," the priest repeated, making a little bridge with his fingers and smiling with his yellow teeth through his thin lips.

Cass decided to stick to the academic version of her story: she was just doing research. It would surely go down easier than trying to sell the whole "race to stop the vampires" version.

"I'm doing my doctoral dissertation on relics related to the One True Cross," Cass began. "We've actually spoken before. A year ago we talked on the phone about some details related to the Chalice of Valencia."

A fat fly buzzed through the open window and spun in leisurely circles around Zach's head. Zach took a couple of swipes at it but missed every time.

Cass gave him an elbow and Miranda shot him a look.

Zach blushed and sat on his hands.

The priest nodded, "Yes, of course. Right. I'm glad you've come. I believe I can help. In fact, I think I've got something that you'll want to see."

Vizzini slowly got to his feet, creaking and groaning. Cass couldn't tell which noises were made by his bones and which were made by the chair.

How old is this guy? He's not going to make it back from the other room.

"Give me just a moment," Vizzini asked as he tottered from the room.

Even though Cass didn't have a great feeling about this, nothing Vizzini had said so far felt like a lie. But she was having a hard time focusing, probably because Miranda was practically sitting in her lap—and she in Zach's. The house was too small to talk privately about anything while Vizzini was out of the room, even if he was hard of hearing. So Cass settled for cocking an eyebrow and sending another questioning glance at Miranda and then Zach. Miranda still looked skeptical. But Cass had a feeling that the bookish research aspect of their adventure wasn't really Miranda's cup of tea anyway. When she gave Zach the same questioning look, he pulled his hands out from between the couch cushions and shrugged.

Right, Cass thought, *you guys are so damn helpful. If I ever need skeptical looks and noncommittal shrugs, I know where to go.*

Zach, though, couldn't keep from smiling.

"Hey," he whispered, "look what I found." He held out a hand and opened it, palm up. He had excavated thirty-seven cents from between the cushions.

What the hell? Cass wondered, adding up the coins in her head.

"And I found this," Zach continued, as he stuffed his other hand back between the cushions to retrieve whatever else he'd discovered.

Cass grabbed his hand before he could pull anything else out of the couch and shot him an angry look.

"No," she whispered fiercely. "Whatever it is, just— no."

Zach let go of whatever he'd found and raised his hands in surrender.

Cass tried to scoot forward onto the edge of the couch and put Zach out of her line of vision.

Vizzini returned and settled back into his creaking chair. He had a small box in his lap. The box was ornate and obviously old.

"This," Vizzini began, "is part of what you're looking for. It only recently came into my possession. Providence, I suppose."

He leaned forward and handed the box to Cass, his hand shaking. Cass accepted it, handling it gently. She examined the sides of the box, noting the array of late medieval iconography that adorned it. She unfastened the delicate clasp that held the box closed and carefully lifted the lid. A puff of stale air escaped from the interior. Inside, nestled in a scarlet red cloth, she found a fragment of wood. Without touching the wood itself, she used the cloth to lift it out of the box and hold it up in the light.

At a glance she could tell that it was the right *kind* of wood and, potentially, the right age. It was exactly the kind of thing she was looking for. But even with Zach squirming next to her, trying to get a look, she could tell that it was a fake.

This fragment of wood was a lie.

Her weak eye twitched and focused. Holding the fragment out in front of her, she met the priest's eyes. With the relic as a focal point, it wasn't hard to see what had been cloudy before.

Shit, Cass realized, *he's lying. He knows this is a fake. He's playing us. But why?*

Cass decidedly immediately, instinctively, to not let on that she knew.

"This is … amazing," Cass offered, careful not to lie, and returned the fragment to its box. She handed the box back to Vizzini. "Does it harbor any clues that might help us track down additional fragments of the One True Cross? Does its presence here in Meliana indicate that there is some truth to the old stories about the Chalice of Valencia?"

The priest smiled his yellow smile again, obviously pleased that Cass seemed to have bought his story. But when she mentioned the Chalice of Valencia, his smile disappeared.

"No, no, not Valencia," he said, a little too quickly. "There's nothing there. The Chalice is not authentic. Don't waste your time with it."

Vizzini paused for a moment, as if debating with himself about what to say next. "I probably shouldn't tell you this," he said, holding the box in his lap protectively, "but if you are serious about finding additional fragments of the Cross, you must visit a small town, just outside of Barcelona, named Montgat."

He continued for several minutes, offering directions, a bit of history, and some reflections on the architecture of the key chapel in Montgat. Cass pretended to carefully note all these additional details.

Even if he's lying, Cass thought, *he's lying in great detail in order to send us someplace quite precise.*

Cass nodded along until he was done, then stood up and thanked him for his time.

On their way out the door, Miranda bobbed her head in gratitude and Cass waved goodbye. Zach, though, stopped, took the priest's hand in both his own, and enthusiastically shook it.

"Thank you, Father. Thank you so much," Zach said. And then, with his crooked grin, dropped the thirty-seven cents he'd found into the priest's hand. "This is for you."

The priest looked at the coins in his hands in bewilderment as Zach skipped off to catch up with Cass and Miranda.

In just a couple of seconds, they were back to the car. Car doors thunked and Richard hit the ignition. The car rumbled to life.

"Well?" Richard said, turning to look at Cass. Zach and Miranda did the same.

"Well," Cass replied, "that was *not* Father Vizzini."

25

ON THE HEELS of Cass's revelation, Richard instinctively stepped on the gas to put some distance between them and the old chapel. He didn't have a particular destination in mind, just somewhere away from here, and now he was driving more like Miranda than even Miranda cared for. Miranda was busy stepping on her imaginary brake instead of her imaginary accelerator.

But unlike Miranda, Richard drove expertly through the narrow streets, deftly cornering and blowing past slower cars.

He probably owns a whole fleet of Formula One cars, Cass thought, then turned her attention back to the business at hand.

"That wasn't Vizzini," Cass started again. "And the relic he showed us was a fake. Just eyeballing the relic, I would have thought it had a shot at being authentic, but then my—powers—kicked in and I could tell that he was lying. In fact, I could tell, somehow, that the *wood* was lying."

Cass couldn't help stumbling over the word *powers*. It sounded ridiculous when she said it out loud. She doubted there would ever be a day when she didn't silently add scare quotes whenever she used the word.

She took a deep breath. She was relieved, though, to be out of that house. She was relieved that Richard had taken her warning seriously and sped them out of there. And she was relieved to have her sword in hand again. They hadn't even been in Vizzini's house for half an hour but, now, she squeezed the sword's grip like she'd just found a long lost friend.

Cass finished her story, filling Richard in about the priest's tip about Barcelona. After she'd finished, everyone was quiet for a minute, digesting the news, until Miranda chimed in.

"If that wasn't Vizzini, then someone went to a lot of trouble to impersonate him. And if that's the case, then Vizzini is probably dead," Miranda said flatly.

This hadn't occurred to Cass but, as soon as Miranda said it, she knew it was probably true. Vizzini was dead. And Cass was, at least in part, responsible: they'd killed him to get at her. Her stomach twisted at the thought.

Richard glanced at Cass in his rearview view and saw her face go green. In response, he downshifted and immediately slipped into an open spot outside a cafe.

"It's time for a break," he said. "And I'd like to check-in with my team about these developments."

Richard claimed a table on the sidewalk and snapped his fingers to catch the attention of the waiter.

In perfect Spanish he rattled off an order of coffee for Zach, Miranda, and himself, and a cup of tea to calm Cass's nerves. Then he made a call with his cell and wandered down the street to conduct the conversation in private.

Cass, Miranda, and Zach took a seat at the table. The mood was somber, but the tea helped soothe her stomach and Zach and Miranda both drained their coffees gratefully.

Richard tucked his phone in his coat pocket and rejoined them.

"It seems, then, like we have two options in continuing our search," Richard proposed. "One, we go look at Valencia Cathedral. Or, two, we head straight to Barcelona and see what we can find there in Montgat. My people agree with our initial assessment: that the Valencia Cathedral is a dead end. However, cross-checking a variety of leads with the instructions given by our fake Father Vizzini has revealed that the site in Montgat is indeed a potential hotspot. If we take some precautions, I think it's worth the risk to check it out. Plus, they don't know that we're onto them, and we might be able to use that to our advantage."

Zach was hesitant. "It smells like a trap. You recognize this and still your advice is to spring it on purpose?"

"Yes," Richard said.

"Using us as bait?"

"No," Richard corrected him, "using *Cassandra* as the bait. Cassandra is all they care about here."

"Right, that makes it much better," Zach countered. "Asshole," he added under his breath, taking another sip of coffee.

Richard's face hardened, but he didn't respond.

Miranda looked like she was leaning toward Richard's idea. She generally preferred an aggressive approach.

Cass, though, wasn't sure about heading to Barcelona. It was true that they'd already ruled out Valencia Cathedral. But there was something about the way the fake priest had been anxious to divert her attention from it that had piqued her curiosity. Her gut said to check it out. Plus, they were already here near Valencia. Why not take a look before driving hours to Barcelona?

Before she even realized that she'd made a decision, Cass said, "We're going to the Cathedral. Then we'll decide from there."

Her words had an air of finality.

She could see that Richard disagreed and that, now, he also itched to make another call. He hadn't expected disagreement but he stayed quiet. Cass admired his self-control.

She didn't trust Richard, exactly. She hadn't yet felt like Richard was lying to her—though, still, she'd also never felt like he was telling her everything. He was holding something back. He was only revealing the bare minimum.

Miranda backed her up. "If Cass says we go to the cathedral, then our next stop is the cathedral."

Zach also agreed, happy to position himself on Cass's side and perhaps even more happy to see Richard not have his way.

"Okay," Richard relented, tossing some money on the table and standing to head back to the car. "Let's go."

But before he could get far from the table, Cass stopped him.

"No," she said. "I'm driving."

She needed Richard's help, but she didn't want him running the show anymore. This was her life on the line, now. She'd be damned if she was going to let someone else be in charge.

She held out her hand, waiting for the keys. Richard dangled them and then reluctantly let them drop into her palm.

"Okay," Cass said, "now let's go."

Richard angled for shotgun, but Miranda cut him off.

"Boys in the back," she said, hiking her thumb.

Cass revved the engine and they were on their way.

God help us, she thought.

26

CASS PARKED A couple of blocks out and they walked the rest of the way. Entering the square from the south, Cass was lost in her own thoughts, worried about the responsibility she'd just claimed for herself, and when she finally looked up she was rocked by the beauty of what she saw. The Valencia Cathedral was stunning. It was built in a predominately Gothic style with blocks of sand-colored stone. Parts of the building dated from the thirteenth century. A sweeping, colonnaded wall buttressed the main entrance.

Cass had read about the cathedral for years and knew its history by heart, but she'd never seen it in person. Her mouth fell open and she accidentally leaned against the arm of whoever happened to be nearest: Richard.

He smiled, squeezed her shoulder, and steadied her.

"You've only seen pictures?" he guessed.

Cass nodded.

"Then it is almost impossible to be prepared. Don't be embarrassed. Take a moment."

Cass did. She took a deep breath and tried to take it in.

Then she tried something else. She closed her eyes, felt for that hint of heat deep behind her cloudy eye, and latched onto it. She opened her eyes and felt her knees go weak again. She leaned harder into Richard's shoulder. The cathedral blazed with a new light, with a beauty that was rooted not just in how it looked but in Cass's deeper vision of what it was.

The cathedral was lit from the inside out. It projected its own halo.

The cathedral was *true*.

God. Damn. How much of the world looks like this? Cass wondered. *How much of this light goes unseen, everyday? How much of it shines in the most ordinary things? How blind are we?*

The longer Cass looked at the cathedral, the more she felt like her own body was saturated with the light. She felt the light lift and strengthen her. She felt calm and powerful. She was reluctant to let go of Richard, but the light surging through her body pulled her toward the door.

You made the right choice, Jones. You're in the right place. There's something here.

Richard, Zach, and Miranda hurried to match Cass's pace.

They paused just inside the narthex. Evening mass was already underway. Cass sighed. They couldn't afford to wait until it had concluded and everyone had emptied out. Cass didn't feel like they had a lot of time to waste—they needed to act now. They needed to slip through the nave unobserved and into the Chapel of the Holy Chalice.

Sensing the reason for Cass's hesitation, Miranda stepped in. "I've got this," she said. Weaving a delicate net of green light with dancing fingers, Miranda said something Cass couldn't quite hear and then cast the net over the four of them.

"Now," she smiled, visibly taxed by the effort, "we're invisible to any prying eyes."

Cass looked at her own hands and at the bodies of her three companions. They didn't look invisible to her, but they were each tinged with a faintly green glow.

"Don't worry. We really are invisible. Just not to anyone included in the spell. But this is difficult for me to do. And it won't last forever. Let's get a move on."

Cass led the way. Even though she knew the cathedral's layout from memory, she wasn't relying on that now. She just followed the light. And the light was, unmistakably, coming from what had to be the Chapel of the Holy Chalice. The four of them moved silently down the length of the nave and into the chapel.

The altar at the head of the Chapel of the Holy Chalice was flanked on both sides by pews. The front wall of the chapel was covered in detailed carvings. At the center of these carvings, the Chalice of Valencia— the cup that Christ himself is said to have used at the Last Supper—was displayed in a glass case.

For Cass, the supernatural light was so strong in the chapel that she almost didn't notice when Richard sat down abruptly. He was shivering, his hands were shaking, and his teeth chattered. He looked sluggish and his lips were blue.

Cass knelt beside him.

"Are you okay, Richard? What's wrong? What's going on?" Cass asked.

"Holy ground," he managed. "It doesn't bar my entry, like the Lost. But passing through it comes with a cost." He held up a shaky, blue hand. "I'm like a snake sliding around on frozen ground."

Cass rubbed his hands between her own, as if she were trying to make a fire.

"Cass," Miranda called, "we need to hurry."

"Yes, please," Richard stuttered.

"I'll take care of this guy," Zach offered, sidling up to Richard on the pew. "Don't you worry about it, Cass."

Then to Richard, "Come here, big guy. You're getting a bear hug."

Richard tried to scoot away, but he ran out of bench. Zach laughed, hugged him close, and rubbed Richard's arms briskly. Zach squeezed Richard's bicep and raised his eyebrows, pretending to be impressed.

Richard was not pleased but, at the moment, there was nowhere to go.

"Here, try this buddy," Zach said, pulling out his lighter and striking a flame. He waved it underneath Richard's chin and then laughed again.

Cass couldn't tell if Richard was suffering more from the sanctified ground or Zach.

"Please, Cassandra. H-h-h-urry," Richard moaned.

Richard was right. It was time to get to work. Cass turned her full attention toward the front of the room where the light shone brightest.

Saturated with light, Cass's normally cloudy eye was clear and sharply focused. She advanced on the front wall, angling toward the display case that contained the chalice. She rounded and approached the altar. She had little doubt, just on the basis of the available scholarship, that the chalice was a fake. But, still, it seemed undeniable that the light was centered on the chalice itself.

As she scanned the stone carvings to the left of the display, her attention snagged on a depiction of the crucifixion. Something was out of place. She traced the shape of the cross with her index finger, from the crown of thorns to the foot of the cross's vertical beam.

There, she thought, *right there.*

She pressed an unusual indentation at the base of the cross and a small, hinged door popped open.

Yessss! Of course! A fragment of the One True Cross, hidden—where else?—in the cross itself!

But when Cass looked inside, she didn't see anything. She poked her finger into the chamber and felt around—nothing. The chamber was empty.

Whatever had been here, they'd already missed it. They were too late.

She didn't know what she'd been thinking. That it would be easy? That they would just waltz in here and find a piece of God, just waiting for them? As if she were special in some way?

Ridiculous, she thought.

She swallowed hard. She'd dared to hope so much so quickly. Hope, she recalled, hurt.

She turned and faced her companions.

"It's not here. It's gone." Cass's voice trailed off. She coughed to hide the tightness in her voice and throat.

Richard was turning an unnatural shade of blue. They needed to get him out of here. He was in bad enough shape that he was actually huddling into Zach's arms, encouraging his embrace. Zach, in turn, had softened a bit. The banter and bravado were gone and his efforts to respond to Richard's obvious need were more genuine. Cuddling on a pew in an ancient cathedral in Spain, they were a striking pair.

Huh, Cass couldn't help thinking, *they actually make a pretty cute couple.*

She flashed on an image of them meandering down the Champs-Élysées in Paris, holding hands and laughing. Then she flashed on an image of them trying to strangle each other beneath the Eiffel Tower.

That's more like it, Cass thought. The darker image matched her darkened mood.

But that didn't really help. And Cass wasn't sure what to do or say next.

Miranda solved that problem for her.

"Holy shit," Miranda said. "What the hell is that?"

27

THEIR HEADS SWIVELED toward Miranda, expecting the worst, but Miranda was pointing at the display case as her voice broke into a high, musical laugh.

"Holy ... shit," Miranda managed again, doubled over with laughter, wiping tears from the corner of her eyes with the back of her hand.

Cass turned to see what Miranda was pointing at: an orange tabby cat was *in* the display case with the Chalice of Valencia, purring and curling around the base of the chalice.

"That's my damn cat," Cass whispered.

She stepped up to the display case and almost pressed her nose to the glass. The cat was wearing a thin black collar and the tag, in a thin cursive script, clearly read "Atlantis."

"That," Cass repeated a second time, "is *my* damn cat."

Richard and Zach looked at each other in disbelief.

"What did she say?" they said almost simultaneously.

Cass couldn't quite bring herself to believe it, either. Of all the crazy things that had happened in the last couple of days, this one seemed a bit too far. Sure, her aunt was a witch, her new crush was a playboy billionaire vampire, and her best friend was desperately in love with her—she could maybe swallow all that. But her cat? Licking the holy grail? Inside a locked display case? In a cathedral blazing with supernatural light? In Spain?

Miranda's laughter still echoed lightly in the chapel. Her makeup was starting to run.

Cass tapped lightly on the glass.

"Here, kitty-kitty," she said. "Here, kitty-kitty-kitty."

Atlantis responded immediately. He turned his attention to Cass, purred, and pressed against the glass opposite her hand. The cat looked Cass square in her weak eye and Cass felt a little jolt that brought the cathedral's additional dimension of light back into sharp focus. Then the cat batted the base on which the chalice was displayed. A second secret compartment popped open—*Sure, why the hell not?*—and Atlantis pawed a fragment of wood out of the slot.

The fragment blazed with so much light Cass was almost blinded.

That, Cass thought, *is a true piece of the One True Cross.*

Richard, Zach, and Miranda were all at her back now, watching.

Cass checked to see if they were seeing what she was seeing. From the stupefied look on their faces, they were. When she looked back at the case, though, the cat was gone. And so was the fragment.

"They have the wrong piece," Cass realized. Whoever beat them to discovering the missing fragment in the first compartment at the foot of the cross, didn't have the real thing.

Cass took a step back, trying to process the implications, and tripped over the cat. Zach dropped Richard like a ton of bricks and gently caught Cass before she hit the floor. He set her back on her feet.

Cass bent down and pulled Atlantis into her arms.

The cat dropped the fragment of wood it was carrying in its mouth into Cass's open hand.

But the moment the blazing fragment touched her bare skin, Cass's body stiffened.

Then she passed out.

28

IT FELT TO Cass like time, rather than dilating, had been short-circuited. It felt like some wires had been crossed. One moment she was plugged-in to the present, the next she was in the past. She had touched the fragment of the cross and then the light blazing from it had crackled blue and enveloped her. She felt it fill her body at a cellular level and then explode in a kind of full-body orgasm.

Holy Mary, Mother of God! Cass thought as she struggled to reassemble the pieces of her mind.

When the light receded and her head had cleared, she found herself in a graveyard. A funeral was underway. She could tell from the way she was positioned in relation to the scene that she was just an observer. Whatever was happening here had already happened. She couldn't act. She couldn't change anything. And she couldn't be seen. She could only watch.

So she watched.

The graveyard was next to a small church. The headstones were crude and many graves—obviously recent—went unmarked. The folk gathered for the funeral were a mix of local dignitaries. The priest overseeing the ceremony looked nervous. Practically everyone had dark hair and dark complexions. Some of the figures—monks?—were hooded.

Alright, Jones, Cass thought to herself, *you've got a decade's worth of training as an archeologist and historian. What can you tell? What can you deduce?*

First question: where are you?

Judging from the climate and terrain, she guessed she wasn't far from Valencia. Probably some place farther east. She could smell the salt air of the Mediterranean Sea. The mix of Latin and colloquial Spanish used by those attending the funeral seemed to confirm this conclusion.

Okay, Jones, Cass decided, *call it Eastern Spain, somewhere on the Mediterranean coast.*

Second question: when are you?

The scene didn't feel remotely contemporary. The spoken Spanish was archaic and the clothing felt like it belonged to the first hundred years or so of the Renaissance.

Okay, Jones, Cass decided again, *call it circa 1500 AD.*

Third question: why are you here? What are you supposed to see? What's the connection with the One True Cross?

This one was tougher. She took a closer look at the faces of the funeral party turned in her direction. She peered at the priest. Nothing stood out to her. She took a closer look at the corpse in its open wooden coffin. The coffin was relatively ornate. The man was dressed in the robes of a Catholic Bishop. No wonder the local elites had shown up.

But what did this have to do with her? Cass took a closer look and her attention was drawn to the plain wooden crucifix the corpse was wearing as a necklace. It was fashioned from an unusual fragment of wood that was clearly not from any trees native to the area. The harder Cass looked at it, the more convinced she was that she could detect a faint glow coming from it.

That's it, Cass thought. *That's what I'm looking for. That is a fragment of the One True Cross. And they buried it with him, in this spot, in this very cemetery.*

As soon as Cass had made this discovery, her connection to the vision began to dim. She could feel its edges growing fuzzy and her own focus weakening. She wasn't sure what it would feel like when the vision ended, so she braced herself.

Nothing spectacular happened, though, the scene just continued to gradually dim.

However, just as her view of this frozen moment was about to shift entirely out of focus, one final detail caught her attention. One of the people in attendance stepped away from the crowd to speak privately with the priest. He was much taller than the priest and, when he removed his hood, he revealed a shock of blond hair.

Wait! Stop! Cass protested, fighting to keep the vision from closing, trying to get a better look.

But it was too late. The vision receded and she woke, as if breaking through the surface of a dream, on the floor of the chapel, her head cradled in Zach's lap.

Her eyes snapped open and Cass immediately sat bolt upright, startling everyone. Then, before anyone could react, she grabbed a fist full of Richard's shirt and pulled him close.

"You!" Cass spat, "You were there!"

29

CASS DESCRIBED THE scene she'd witnessed and Richard agreed: he had been there.

Zach and Miranda looked on, confused.

"What is going on, Cass?" Zach asked. "What are you talking about? What happened to you?"

Cass ignored him. Richard had her full attention. She held his eyes.

"Did you know?" Cass asked. "Did you know that the Bishop in the cemetery was buried with a piece of the One True Cross?"

Richard glanced away and then back again, as if he were still trying to decide how much to tell her.

"I suspected," Richard admitted, his lips still blue, his hands still shaking. "The true importance of such relics only became clear to me later on. At the time, it seemed like a good idea to just keep such things out of circulation and away from hungry eyes." He paused then started again. "I wasn't sure what it was, but I was happy to have it buried."

Cass weighed his response. As usual, he wasn't lying. But, as usual, she wasn't sure that what he'd said added up to the whole truth.

"Cassandra," Richard continued, "if we're done here, c-c-could we continue this conversation outside?" He gestured toward the door, already shuffling that way.

Were they done here, Cass wondered? The fragment of the Cross delivered by Atlantis was still in her hand. She looked around the room for the cat but, of course, he was lost again—at least to her. At this point, though, after saving her life and tracking down a fragment of the divine, she doubted that Atlantis was ever lost to himself.

If there was something left to do here, she couldn't see it.

The three of them filed out of the chapel behind Richard. Miranda, visibly weakened by the earlier strain of keeping them hidden, was last out the door. Evening Mass had concluded though, and the nave was empty so there was no longer any need to hide.

The closer they got to the door, the better Richard looked. Cass could almost visibly see his strength returning, his posture improving, until he pushed with both hands through the exterior double doors and burst out into the night. Once he was out into the open air, he tilted his head back, took a deep breath, and looked deep into the night sky. He claimed to be unaffected by daylight but he never looked like this in the sun. He never looked ... *at home* like he did here, in the night. Now that she'd spent a day with him, Cass could spot the difference easily. Richard rolled his shoulders, still drinking in the stars, and, for just a moment, Cass thought he was going to howl at the moon. But he didn't.

Instead, pale and powerful in the dark, he turned back to her.

Zach had joined them. He could see the difference, too. He bristled and stepped protectively between them. He obviously preferred his vampires frozen, blue, and supine.

"Cass," Zach started, glancing at Richard over her shoulder, "I think it's time to seriously consider continuing this little adventure without the assistance of any ... playboys."

Richard didn't look faintly threatened by Zach or by his proposal. He just looked right past Zach at Cass and gently raised an eyebrow.

Cass didn't need any macho posturing from Richard at the moment. And she definitely didn't need protection from Zach. What she needed was answers and Richard—not Zach—was the only one who had them.

"Miranda," Cass said simply, holding Richard's gaze. "Take Zach with you back to the car. Richard and I need to talk."

Zach was about to protest, but he couldn't tell whether this meant she might be taking his idea seriously.

"Cass—" Zach began.

"Not now, Zach," Cass interrupted. "Just go with Miranda. Please."

Zach had known Cass long enough to know when to let something go. He gathered up Miranda and they headed back to the car. Miranda looked relieved that she would have a chance to sit down.

Now it was just Cass and Richard in the square.

"Let's walk," Cass said. "I have some questions."

Richard nodded and they set off at a meandering pace. Cass pulled the band from her ponytail and let her hair fall. She stuffed her hands in the pockets of her jeans. She felt ordinary and small next to Richard. Richard shrugged out of his jacket and draped it over her shoulders.

For the first couple of minutes, they just walked in silence.

"You really *were* born in the fifteenth century," Cass offered.

"Around there," Richard confirmed.

"You've been walking the face of the planet for six hundred years?"

"Yes," he said, keeping his gaze fixed on the sidewalk in front of them.

"Shit," she said.

"Correct."

They rounded a corner, headed deeper now into a residential area.

Richard picked up the thread on his own. "In this case, in your vision, I was in Barcelona—on assignment. Those in power at that time saw my gifts as unholy, but that didn't prevent them from using me. I was sent to investigate what was happening with the Inquisition in

Montgat. Rumors had spread to Barcelona that the Holy Inquisition had, in that town, taken an unholy turn."

Flapping in the evening breeze, Richard's oversized jacket slipped from Cass's shoulder. Richard tugged it back into place and gently swept Cass's black hair out from underneath its collar with the back of his hand.

Cass pulled the coat tight around her.

"And …?" she prompted.

"And the rumors were true. Lost vampires had infiltrated the Inquisition in Montgat, bending it to their own ends. The Bishop himself was not a vampire but he was at the heart of the trouble. He'd come into possession of a powerful relic that, in its fragmentary state, was easily abused. It was my job to clean up the mess. So I dispensed with the vampires, poisoned the bishop, and saw to it that he was buried with the relic."

It was Cass's turn to stare at the sidewalk ahead, not meeting Richard's eyes.

"Okay," she said. "I believe you. But now we've got three independent lines of evidence intersecting: the planted clue from the fake Vizzini, my vision, and your memory. I don't see that we've got much choice now but to go to Montgat and spring the trap."

"I'm afraid you may be right," Richard agreed. "And we'll need to hurry. My team has only recently confirmed that a shadowy figure long suspected of funding and directing a variety of corrupt enterprises is behind this race to collect all the available fragments of the Cross. In addition to the fragment we possess, all he needs now is the fragment known as the anointed piece."

"The anointed piece … a fragment of the Cross that actually bears the blood of Christ's own body."

"Yes. That's right. And this man—he goes by many names—is assuredly a vampire. Some even claim that he was the first to bear the curse and that, in one way or another, every vampire since is a descendant of his."

Excellent, Cass thought. *Way to take things slow, Jones, and work your way up to the big boss. First time out and you're taking on the baddest ass of them all.*

Cass had stopped walking. They'd gone in a circle and were almost back to the square, but the street they were on was still quiet, poorly lit, and residential.

Richard leaned against the wall of a house.

Cass looked him up and down. Could she trust him? Did she have a choice?

"Six hundred years is a long time," she said.

"It is a very long time," Richard allowed.

Seeing Richard backlit by his deep past, he suddenly looked very tired and very lonely to Cass. And seeing him this way, Cass suddenly felt very tired and very lonely herself.

Her eye felt weak and her body ordinary.

The road ahead looked rocky.

As Richard turned his head to watch a small car crawl by, Cass stepped in close, slid her hand behind his neck, and pulled his face down to hers. She kissed him full on the mouth, parting his lips with her tongue, hungry to not feel alone. She needed to taste the salt on him. Richard was surprised, but when she pressed her body tight against his, he put his hands low on her hips and pulled her even closer.

When Cass pulled back to catch her breath, he tenderly tucked her hair behind her ear. But when, after a moment, he leaned in to kiss her again, Cass put her hands on his chest and held him at arm's length.

"That's all," she said, handing him back his jacket. "That's all for now."

Then she took Richard's hand and pulled him toward the square.

"Hurry," she said. "We've got to get to Barcelona."

30

THE THIN MAN was not pleased.

He was home, now, in his castle in Romania. He'd lived here for centuries. The castle was remote and secluded and the rooms were dry, cold, and dark, just as he preferred. But, at the moment, this did not soothe him.

Three of his colleagues stood nervously near the room's entrance. The thin man was, as usual, quiet and reserved. But even standing still behind his glass desk, he gave the impression that something was about to explode.

He'd watched the whole series of events that unfolded in the Chapel of the Holy Chalice via a handful of tiny, strategically placed cameras. The footage was open on his desktop monitor. He rewound the video for the eleventh time and watched again the segment that showed Cass finding the empty compartment, the appearance of the cat, the discovery of the true fragment, and Cass's collapse.

His men had been there first. They'd arrived at the chapel before Cass and claimed the fragment of wood hidden in the carving of the cross. His colleagues, however, hadn't be able to tell that it was a fake. Now Cass and company had the real fragment and he had a paperweight.

He rewound the footage twice more, looking for any important details he might have missed. Halfway through the second time he had to sit down abruptly in his office chair. A shooting pain in his right leg almost sent him tumbling to the floor. His colleagues looked on, pretending not to notice, but they were obviously weighing the meaning of these developments.

The cloud of black flesh had advanced all the way up his arm, down his side, and into his leg. It was starting to spread across his chest and up his neck.

For more than two thousand years now he'd walked the earth. For more than two thousand years he had ranged up and down across its face, from the Sea of Galilee to Rome to China and back, bearing the weight of his curse.

The thin man felt his rage boil over.

His anger propelled him back onto his feet.

"You," he pointed, "you brought back this useless decoy?"

He snatched the fragment of wood from his desk and held it up to the light, as if examining its authenticity.

His colleague swallowed hard and nodded his head.

Then, without warning, the thin man vaulted across his desk, ignoring the pain in his arm and leg, and decapitated the man with a single, herculean twist of his neck. What was left of the man turned to ash in his hands.

The remaining two scuttled out of the way, terrified by his volcanic shift from reserved to homicidal.

Good, the thin man thought. *The loss is regrettable but, in addition to venting my frustration, this may help keep order in their ranks a bit longer. They'll be second guessing how weak I have or haven't become. Their loyalty needs to hold fast just a bit longer. I can't allow them to be tempted by the Heretic or her splinter group of Lost vampires. Acquiring the remaining relics may not heal me, but it will cement my control over them.*

"Do not fail me," he said to the two that remained. "The punishment will be swift and harsh. Too much is at stake. For now, get out."

They hesitated for a moment.

"Leave!" he commanded, lowering his voice and shifting its register. And they were gone.

The thin man slammed the door behind them and then hobbled over to his desk. He rewound the video again, this time freezing an image of Cass's face as she snapped back awake after her vision.

What did you see? he wondered. *Where did you go? And what does it have to do with Richard York?*

He was curious, but in some respects it didn't matter. Even their failure in the Chapel of the Holy Chalice was only a minor setback. Cass had the true fragment in her possession. Just knowing where it was—knowing that she had it—was enough. He would take it from her when the time came.

And, even more importantly, his scouts had reported that she and her friends were already headed to Barcelona. They would arrive around midnight. And then, intentionally or not, they would lead him to the location of the final piece of the puzzle: the anointed piece.

Together with the fragments of the One True Cross he had already collected, the anointed piece would exponentially expand the scope of his power and, crucially, heal him.

He touched the frozen image of Cassandra Jones with his black hand.

"Thank you, dear girl, for helping me."

31

IT WAS HALF past midnight when they stopped in front of a small chapel in Montgat.

Zach had driven them from Valencia. Miranda had claimed the front seat and closed her eyes as soon as they hit the freeway. Richard and Cass took the backseat.

Both Richard and Cass now knew what they were looking for, but neither was certain where to locate the church. After half an hour of sorting through her notes and maps with Richard, then cross-referencing this information with the so-called Father Vizzini's speculations and the details Cass and Richard knew first-hand, Cass settled on the most likely location.

Once this was done, Cass was exhausted. Her body had no idea what time it was. Jet-lag was catching up to her. She tried to fight it, but eventually she closed her eyes and rested her head on Richard's shoulder. Right before she dozed off she glanced up towards the rearview mirror to see Zach glancing back at them, his knuckles white on the steering wheel.

When the car finally stopped, Cass woke up, embarrassed by the drool she'd left on Richard's shoulder.

Great, Jones, now you're literally drooling on the man. Have a little dignity.

She smiled weakly in Richard's direction and hopped out of the car.

The chapel was old—dating from the thirteenth century—but well preserved. More, it sat against the type of hill they expected.

Cass led the way. It was dark and the site was poorly lit. This time she didn't hesitate to bring her mother's sword. Part of her ached to swing the sword and feel its perfect balance and supernatural edge cut through whatever obstacles they might face—and part of her wanted nothing more than to go home, lock it in a closet, and never take it out again.

As far as any of them could see, they were alone. But, despite what their eyes indicated, it didn't *feel* to Cass like they were alone. It felt like the chapel was watching them.

They made their way around to the side of the building. Unlike in Valencia, they weren't interested in the chapel itself. They were interested in the adjoining graveyard. They were looking for the crypt where Richard's poisoned Bishop was buried. The fake Vizzini had pointed them in this general direction, but he hadn't been able to say exactly where to look or how to find the relic. Without some concrete clues, they'd be looking for a needle in a haystack.

But this was, after all, why they—well, Richard and the mystery person who had texted her—needed Cass. They might be able to narrow down the possibilities, but they needed her to get them across the finish line.

Fine, Cass thought, *I've been playing Indiana Jones in the backyard since I was five. I can do the real thing now.*

She glanced at Zach. "Let's go."

Then, before he could respond, she opened the gate.

The graveyard was tucked up against the side of the chapel. But it was small, much smaller than Cass had expected, and hemmed in by a relatively modern wrought iron fence. Some of the headstones were hundreds of years old, but most of them only dated from the 1800s. Doubtless, bodies had been buried on top of bodies for generations in this yard, but there weren't any crypts in sight.

"Damn," Cass said under her breath. "This is close, but it's *not* what we're looking for. A lot can change in six hundred years and the chapel feels right, but this isn't the graveyard I saw in my vision."

"I agree," Richard said, kicking at a loose stone.

Miranda was hanging back near the entrance, keeping an eye on the street. Zach, meanwhile, had already wandered clear to the back of the yard. When he reached the fence, he swung himself over the top with a casual strength and kept walking.

"Zach," Cass called.

Zach didn't respond. He just kept walking.

Cass followed and jumped the fence herself. She followed him into the deeper darkness of the overgrown hill behind the chapel. He continued on about a hundred yards and then stopped. When she caught up with him, he touched her arm and pointed.

"There," Zach said. "Do you see it?"

At first Cass couldn't make anything out. But when she leaned in closer and looked straight down the length of Zach's arm, she saw what he was pointing at: the ruins of a sprawling, forgotten graveyard were scattered through the tall grass and clumps of trees that covered the hillside.

Richard joined them. In the woods, at night, he moved without making a sound. When he spoke, Zach jumped, surprised.

"This is it," Richard said, placing his hand in the small of Cass's back. "This is the place we're looking for."

Cass nodded as she leaned back, just a hair, into his touch.

"Yes," she confirmed, "yes it is."

"Of course it is," Zach interjected. "That's why I pointed it out. And also," he waved his hand at the ground in front of them, "that's why there's a big X marking the spot."

Cass looked down, squeaked, and took a startled step back, bumping into Richard. She had to cover her mouth to stifle a laugh.

They *were* practically standing on the granite ruins of a headstone, shaped like an X.

"Close," Cass said. "But it's not quite an X."

She grabbed Zach by the shoulders and moved him forty-five degrees to the right, until they were both looking right down the length of the X's longest side.

"It's better than an X. It's a cross. And it's pointing straight ahead."

Cass pushed through the underbrush, ignoring the thorns. The broken headstone wasn't magic, but it had orientated her to the shape of the hill and she could see, now, how to superimpose what she'd seen in her vision onto the ground in front of them.

The crypt they were looking for should be about thirty yards ahead, just to the left. Even though she kept her eyes peeled for any indication that she was on the right track, she still almost walked right past the crypt itself. The small structure lay in ruins, overgrown with weeds and almost reclaimed by the earth.

"Over here!" she called, unable to contain her excitement.

She cleared some of the brush and located the door.

She was about to grab the handle and give it a heave when a voice from the darkness interrupted her. Was it coming from the sky? Was God speaking to her?

No, it was coming from the trees.

"Thank you for your help," the voice said. "Our master will be very pleased."

And then, before Cass could react, the trees came alive and a score of vampires leapt from their branches.

32

CASS'S FIRST THOUGHT—God help her—was to wonder if European vampires also dressed exclusively in black leather.

As the group's leader fluttered to the ground in front of her in a long, black, leather trench coat, she was glad to see that a minor shift from the American-biker-gang vibe to an upscale-Italian-leather vibe hadn't broken with the underlying trend. She appreciated consistency.

Okay, Jones, you can handle this. Just do what you did before.

Nineteen other vampires dropped from the trees, surrounding them.

Times twenty.

Without thinking, Cass reacted reflexively. The sword felt true in her hand as she took the offensive, sending the trench coat vampire spinning out of the way with a handful of opening strokes. As he spun, though, his coat flared dramatically, fanning out around him.

And that *is why you don't wear a trench coat to a sword fight*, Cass thought.

She grabbed the coat's long tail with her free hand, yanked the vampire back within the arc of her sword, and lopped off his head. Both head and body spontaneously dissolved into ash. The sword was so sharp, Cass barely felt any resistance as it sliced through meat and bone.

Having drawn first blood, the sword came alive in her hand. It shone with a smoky, white light that drifted upward off the blade. Cass could feel the light penetrate deep into the bones of her right hand and spread from the blade up her arm and into her heart, lungs, and head. Her weak eye focused and cleared and time expanded again, giving her room to see the truth and react to it. Her mother's necklace glowed white hot between her breasts. From Cass's point of view, the whole hillside was flooded with this same white light. The crypt she'd uncovered pulsed like a beacon. She could see the whole scene with perfect clarity.

"Uhh, Cass," Zach said, touching her elbow. "Your eyes are ... uh ... burning? With light?

Cass cleared her throat.

"Right," she said, as if she'd expected that all along.

She shrugged off her jacket and tossed it to one side.

"Which one of you is in charge now?" she asked, brandishing the sword.

The only response was some scattered hissing and a lot of scurrying around.

"Right," she said. "It doesn't really matter, does it?"

Before all hell could break loose, Cass tried to take stock of where Richard, Zach, and Miranda were positioned. Watching out for them—especially Zach, who even now sported an inappropriately dopey grin—was going to complicate matters.

She tried to position herself defensively between Zach and the nearest vampire and did a double-take when she saw that Zach was sporting a pair of heavy oak truncheons. The business end of each truncheon was whittled to a sharp point and perpendicular handles were positioned about a third of the way down the shaft. They looked old, heavy, and unbreakable. And Zach spun them like he knew what he was doing.

Where the hell did my mild mannered friend from work go?

A vampire dressed in some kind of s-and-m fetish outfit launched itself at Zach. Cass moved to intercept it but was waylaid by two more coming from the other side. Zach, though, didn't really need her help. He sidestepped the attack, clocked the guy in the head with a skull-cracking blow, and staked him in the heart just below his nipple ring.

Ash.

Cass was busy lopping an arm off one assailant and beheading the other, but she'd seen the whole sequence.

"Uhh, Zach," Cass said.

"Yeah?"

"You're a badass?"

"Uhh, yeah."

"Right," Cass concluded.

Things devolved quickly from there. The vampires decided their best tactic would be to just overrun the four of them with superior numbers.

Miranda didn't look to be at her best but the green spell she wove and shouted was strong. She cast a shimmering green field around the four of them that their attackers had to fight through to reach them.

"Brilliant," Cass called. Now they could deal with just a couple at a time while the others were still fighting their way through.

It didn't take long, though, for company to start arriving.

Cass dispatched a pair of vampires—in *matching* leather pants and vests?—as they were still fighting through the wall.

One head, two heads. Ash.

But while she was doing this, three others made it inside. Miranda couldn't help on this front. It took everything she had to keep the wall up.

Two of them went straight for Richard, one for Cass.

Richard leaned down and picked up a fist-sized stone, tossing it casually in the air with one hand. As the vampires closed, he grabbed the first by the shirt, swung him to the ground, and jumped off his back into the air. With the full force of gravity added to his strength, Richard punched down into the face of the other one with his rock, breaking bones. The vampire was stunned but not down. But before Richard could take advantage of his dazed state, the first vampire swept his legs out from under him and pinned him to the ground. He absorbed a couple of blows from Richard but kept him pinned. He was trying to get a grip on Richard's head, but Richard bucked and squirmed.

As soon as the second one recovered, Richard would be in big trouble. Cass could already see the second one coming out of the corner of her eye when the vampire dissolved into a shower of ash to reveal Zach standing behind him. Zach had staked him in the heart from behind.

With a running start, Zach kicked the other in the head and sent him tumbling, freeing Richard. Richard scrambled, caught the vampire's ankles, and held him down while Zach delivered the final blow. Another pile of ash.

"Thank you," Richard rasped.

"You're welcome," Zach said, but then couldn't stop himself from adding. "Asshole." He extended a hand and helped Richard to his feet, then said in his ear, "And if you hurt her—in any way—I will do the same to you."

Richard swallowed his first, angry response, and just nodded.

Gripping Zach by the shoulder he said again, "Thank you. And if *you* hurt her, I'll do the same."

"Fellas," Cass called. "If you're done bonding now, I could use a little help over here."

Cass had called for some help, but it didn't especially look like she needed it. Her sword flashed, the light poured off her like smoke, and she moved with uncanny speed and anticipation. A lifetime of training and her newly awakened gifts converged. Vampires were dropping like flies.

Miranda, though, was fading. Every ounce of her concentration was directed at maintaining the wall and she appeared to be totally oblivious to what was happening immediately around her.

Cass dispatched two vampires that were headed for Miranda. But the idea caught on and pretty soon every vampire through the wall was aiming for her. Cass struggled to fend them off but when one got too close, Cass was bumped into Miranda's magic wall, with her sword hand trapped in its green, molasses light.

"Cassandra!" Richard called.

Zach took over the job of defending Miranda and Richard rushed to help Cass. Taking a cue from Cass's own predicament, he shoved a vampire angling for Cass into the wall and trapped him there.

"Cass," Richard said, taking her free hand. "Do you trust me?"

Cass hesitated for a moment, just as she had last time, and wondered if she truly did. She felt her connection to her power flicker in response.

What if you get the answer wrong, Jones? What if you don't even know what you really think?

A look of regret flashed across Richard's face as he registered her hesitation.

Screw it, Cass thought, *trust isn't a fact like a rock, it's a choice.*

"I trust you," she said. And she was telling the truth.

Her power flared in a blaze of white light. Richard let go of her hand, grabbed a heavy tree branch off the ground, and swung right for Miranda's head, knocking her unconscious. Miranda collapsed in a heap and the wall collapsed with her.

Cass was free.

There were only a handful of vampires left now and in a whirlwind of light and ash Cass finished them off.

Richard and Zach both just watched, frozen in place by the sheer destructive beauty of Cass's movements.

Once she was done, though, Cass went straight for Miranda. She cradled her head.

"Miranda," Cass whispered. "Miranda, can you hear me?"

Miranda didn't stir. She lay limp in Cass's arms.

"Miranda," she called again, wiping away tears with the heel of her hand.

Cass bent over and touched her forehead to Miranda's and, when she did, her necklace, still glowing white, swung free of her shirt and brushed Miranda's cheek.

Miranda's eyes snapped open.

"Are we safe?" she asked.

"Yes," Cass said, "we're safe. Thanks to you."

33

RICHARD GRABBED HOLD of the door to the crypt and gave it a pull. It didn't budge. It was stuck fast. So he took off his jacket and rolled up his sleeves.

"You're literally rolling up your sleeves," Cass teased.

"Yes," he said. Glancing back over his shoulder, he added defensively, "It's a very *English* thing to do."

He planted his feet wide at the base of the door, grabbed the handle with both hands, and pulled again. For a moment, nothing happened—nothing except his shoulders and biceps straining against the fabric of his shirt. Then he tore the whole door from its hinges and tossed it aside.

Zach busied himself steadying Miranda and pretended not to notice that feat of strength.

Where the door had been, a dark hole in the ground opened like a mouth onto a set of stairs that descended into the crypt.

Cass exchanged looks with Zach, then Miranda, then Richard. They all silently agreed that there was nothing to be done now but descend into the darkness.

She was worried, though, about what might be waiting for them down there.

What if there are werewolves down there, Jones, she thought. *Are werewolves a thing? Would Miranda and Richard laugh at her if she brought it up, as if she were somehow supposed to know that witches and vampires were real but that, of course, werewolves were totally imaginary? And what about leprechauns? Or unicorns? Were those a thing?*

That train of thought was going nowhere, so Cass let it go and turned back to the business at hand.

"Zach, stay here with Miranda and rest for a few minutes. There's no reason to haul you both into the dark with me."

Zach wanted to disagree but, feeling Miranda's weight lean against him, he bit his tongue.

Miranda, on the other hand, just looked grateful.

Then Cass looked squarely at Richard.

"You, though," she said, "are expendable. You're coming with me."

They started to go, but Zach interrupted them.

"Wait," Zach said, holding out a truncheon to Richard, "take this."

Richard nodded and accepted it gratefully.

Cass led the way into the dark. Her powers had cooled, but she still gave off a faint glow. And, in particular, her mother's blade and necklace left a wispy trail of light as she descended the steps. Richard stayed close behind. Cass turned on her phone's flashlight app and Richard did the same.

They only had to descend half a flight of stairs until they'd reached the floor of the crypt itself.

In the center of the floor, there was a heavy stone box containing the bishop's coffin. Apart from the box, there wasn't much else to see.

To Cass's eyes, the pulsing light of the crypt was less dramatic now than it had been earlier, but the box was definitely its epicenter. And the closer they got, the more obvious it was to Cass that her pendant was pulsing in sync.

Richard moved to slide the stone lid off the box, but a cross was chiseled into the length of it. Cass saw him waver and took the initiative, pushing hard until the lid slid off with a rumbling groan. Reaching inside the box, she lifted the coffin lid and there, in all his rotted glory, was the one-time bishop of Montgat. And there, around his neck, was the relic that she'd seen in her vision.

She leaned in and, with a handkerchief, lifted it from the coffin, the string from which it had hung disintegrating in her hands. She held it up in the light for Richard to see.

"This is the real thing," Cass affirmed, though she could hardly believe it. In forty-eight hours she'd gone from having an abandoned and discredited dissertation about Christian relics to having, in her personal possession, *two* authentic fragments of the One True Cross.

Richard pulled their first fragment, the piece from the Chapel of the Holy Chalice, out of his pocket. It was locked inside a clear, shatterproof vial. He held them up side by side. The fragments vibrated in concert when he held them close together and, even at a glance, there was no doubt they were made from the same distinctive wood.

"You did it, Cass," Richard said. "Your talents and research brought us here. You were the key. You were right all along."

The words hit Cass hard. She'd fought through so much doubt and disappointment just to stay afloat this past year. And now—here, half-way around the world —the thing she'd dreamed about deep in the stacks of her father's library had come true. The thing she'd dreamed was real.

She felt like her heart would burst.

This, though, was tempered by a pang of sadness that her father couldn't be here to see it, to share it with her. He was one of the few people in the world who would appreciate the magnitude of what she'd done. But, feeling the weight of her mother's blade in her hand, she was grateful, too, that he'd (almost) given his blessing when they'd parted.

Richard touched her shoulder.

"Cassandra, we should go."

"Yes …" she said, stalling.

"What is it?" Richard asked.

Cass took the vial from Richard and held it together with the fragment in her own hand. She turned them both over, carefully examining the fragments from every angle. Then she saw it. She saw what was missing.

"Richard," she began, "neither of these fragments has any blood stains. This fragment we found with the bishop is *not* the anointed piece. We were wrong."

What little blood there was in Richard's face drained right out of it.

"What?" Cass asked.

"Hurry. Let's go," Richard said rushing them back up the stairs.

When they reached the surface again, Cass called out excitedly for Zach and Miranda.

But Zach and Miranda were nowhere to be seen.

Cass felt a deep, black panic well up in her throat.

"Zach!" she yelled, "Miranda!"

Richard echoed her.

"Zach! Miranda!"

Nothing.

Cass was trying to get far enough outside of her panic to think straight when her phone buzzed in her pocket. She dug it out.

She had a text.

It was from the same number that had texted her days ago. The same number that had set this whole sequence of events in motion with that first, cryptic, out-of-the-blue message: "I've read your dissertation. We need to talk."

There was nothing cryptic about this new message, though.

This time the message was crystal clear.

I have your friends.

Bring the fragments to the following coordinates by midnight tomorrow.

Tell no one.

Or they will die.

34

"IT'S *HIM*," RICHARD said. "The leader of the Lost. And he'll do it."

"No," Cass said quietly, more to herself than Richard. She was gripped by a second wave of panic and, when this receded, she was flooded with a wave of anger so fierce it felt like her skin was on fire. Her face flashed red. Only the knuckles throttling her sword were white.

This wasn't helpful, though.

Even the anger.

At least, not yet.

For now, she needed a clear head. And a plan. And, as the coordinates indicated, a way to get to Romania.

At least money was no obstacle. Richard routed his personal jet to Barcelona. They met the plane at the airport and within two hours were in the air. They couldn't fly directly to Romania, though. They needed to conceal their true destination, even from Richard's friends. They couldn't risk it. So they flew to Istanbul, left their phones on the plane, and used cash to buy a pair of train tickets to Bucharest.

The train would take most of the day but they wouldn't have any trouble arriving before midnight. They bought tickets for a private cabin and hoped, before arriving, to find a few hours to rest.

The cabin was comfortable but small. They pulled the blinds to blot out the sun and sat side by side in the shadows, listening in silence to the clack of the rails.

Neither said anything.

There was nothing to say.

But the silence didn't feel hostile. Instead, working a notch below words, it opened a connection between them.

Richard, Cass could tell, was no stranger to silence. He knew how to sit with it. She had no trouble imagining that he'd spent some part of the past six hundred years locked away in a dungeon or monastery, bound by silence for years at a time.

She gauged his profile in the half light and tried to recall what he'd looked like in her vision: the hood, the less guarded look on his face, the beard.

He noticed her looking and, bowing his head, squeezed her hand.

The gesture was simple. And true. Tears welled in Cass's eyes.

"Shhhh," Richard said. He put his arm around her and pulled her close, cradling her head in the hollow of his shoulder.

They sat this way for a long time, his arm wrapped around her shoulder, her hand resting lightly on his chest. The rocking of the train was soothing.

Gradually, it dawned on Cass that, though her hand lay right over Richard's heart, she couldn't feel it beating. She lifted her head from his shoulder, trying to get a better look at him and pressed her hand more firmly against his heart.

Nothing.

Cass sat up straight, swung her leg across his lap, and straddled him. She needed to see his face. She needed to look him in the eye.

Richard, as if he were ashamed at what she'd discovered, kept his gaze downcast.

She responded by taking his head in her small hands and kissing his forehead, just barely grazing his skin with her lips. She softly kissed his temples and his eyes and his ears and trailed down his neck to the open collar of his shirt and the notch of his collarbone.

"Cassandra," he said.

"Shhhh," she said, straining to listen.

She unbuttoned his shirt, slowly and carefully. She traced a wicked scar across his breast and then placed her ear directly against his heart. A flicker of heat deep behind her weak eye emptied her mind, time slowed to a crawl, the sounds of the train disappeared, and she listened with an intensity she'd never managed before.

Her head rose and fell against his chest with the air in his lungs.

She placed a finger lightly on his neck, right against his jugular.

And then—there, deep inside the cavity of his chest —she heard it. An extraordinarily faint and irregular heartbeat.

Part of him was still alive.

A whistle blew and the train began to slow.

They were already there.

35

FROM THE TRAIN, they took a taxi up into the mountains. The taxi let them off at the end of a long, gated driveway that wound upward through a thick forest. From there, they walked. The air was cold. The night sky was clear. And, this far from any lights, the stars were sharp and bright.

Once they were a mile or so up the drive, Richard tossed the large canvas bag he'd been carrying onto the shoulder of the driveway. It clanked and rattled.

Richard had cobbled together some supplies.

In the shadow of the trees lining the drive, they stripped out of their street clothes and into something more tactical: uniformly dark clothes and good boots, all of it designed to maximize their freedom of movement.

When it came to their gear, Cass only had two rules: no corsets and no leather of any kind.

"I agree that they're not a good fit for the occasion," Richard observed dryly, "but there's no need to make such hard and fast rules."

Cass considered his objection.

"Let me add a single exception to that rule, then," she said, retrieving her sword from the canvas bag. "Corsets and bustiers may be worn on special occasions —but only if *everyone* present is similarly dressed."

Her mother's blade whistled and flashed in the starlight as she tested its weight in her hand. Then she turned back toward Richard with the sword pointed casually in his direction.

He looked at the blade and back to Cass. "Excellent rule," he said. "Well thought out. I'm one hundred percent on board."

Richard reached into the bag and retrieved Zach's modified truncheons, both the one that he'd given to Richard and the one that had been left at the crypt. He tucked them into his belt and tossed the bag with their street clothes into the woods.

They had about two miles left to go. The driveway rose steeply and once they'd reached a decisive bend in the road, their destination came into view.

A castle, Cass thought, incredulous. *A goddamn Romanian castle. I should have known.*

"Now what?" Richard asked.

"They know we're coming. And if we don't appear in the next hour, we're risking Zach's and Miranda's lives. There's nothing to do but walk right up the drive and knock on the front door."

It took about twenty minutes to reach the main door. When they arrived, Richard did as Cass had suggested. He knocked on the enormous wooden door. They could hear the sound echo through the space behind it.

They only had to wait a few moments until the door groaned open. Despite the courtly ambiance, the man who opened the door looked more like a goon than a butler. In fact, none of the assembled welcoming committee would have passed on *Downton Abbey*.

But, just as Cass was thinking this, the group parted and revealed a thin man dressed in an impeccable suit. Except for the cloud of black flesh seeping up the right side of his face, *he* might very well have passed as a duke or a count.

Surely, Cass mused, *this guy* must *be an actual count. If he's not Count of the Lost (or whatever), I'm Joan of Arc.*

The thin man stepped forward, unfazed by the naked blade in Cass's hand.

"Please," he said, "come in. It's so rare that we have guests here. Just, please—for the sake of your own friends—check your weapons with my … colleagues here."

Richard hesitated but Cass sheathed her sword, stepped across the threshold, and handed it to one of the goons as if he were checking coats.

The thin man clapped his hands and laughed to see her respond with such civility.

"Excellent, excellent," he said, drinking her in. "You have turned out to be so much more than I'd ever dared hope. We've been through so much together the past few days, I feel like we've been friends for years."

Cass smiled an obviously fake smile. The well-dressed man smiled back and tried to make eye contact, but was foiled by her weak eye. He wasn't sure where to look, so—like most everyone Cass had ever met—he simply broke off trying.

The gaunt man turned on his heel, coughing into his gloved fist. Even from six feet away, Cass could see flecks of blood.

Richard was still lingering at the door.

"And, of course, you are not alone."

Richard scowled.

"Hello, Richard," the thin man said, directing a wink at Cass.

The way he said it, Cass couldn't help but think that he and Richard had already met.

She was right.

"Hello, Judas," Richard replied.

36

Despite the veneer of hospitality, they were prisoners.

Judas's men herded them through a maze of corridors to the castle's solar. The room had high, vaulted ceilings and was dominated at one end by a massive fireplace and on the other by a series of desks and museum-grade storage units for artifacts.

Normally, Cass would have been fascinated by both the castle and the high-tech gear. But her fear for Zach and Miranda sat like a rock in the pit of her stomach. When she saw both Zach and Miranda bound and unconscious on the floor she felt simultaneously relieved and infuriated. It was a weird cocktail of emotions.

Cass and Richard were shoved into a pair of wooden chairs and handcuffed to the legs.

Judas was smooth. Everything he did was measured. He seemed calm and in control. But every minute or so he would suffer a painful convulsion that would crack that facade, contorting his blackened face, and reveal how deeply he was suffering.

"I believe you've brought me something," Judas said to Cass.

He approached Cass's chair.

"I'm grateful that you were willing to travel around the world to assist me. Your initial response seemed less open to helping."

He circled around them, behind Richard's chair, and rested a hand on Richard's shoulder as if they were friends.

"I suspected, though, that a dashing man of international mystery like Mr. York here would pique your interest in a way that I never could. Once I'd baited him with some carefully planted warnings and clues, I knew he'd be able to hook you. So thank you both for your help—however unwitting. I couldn't have done it without you."

Cass rattled her cuffs angrily—and uselessly—against the chair. Her wrists were already bruised and bleeding from straining against them.

"Now, where is it?" he asked, circling and staring intently at Cass.

Cass remained silent but, for just a moment, glanced involuntarily at Richard.

"Of course," Judas said, approaching Richard. He studied Richard for a moment and took in his bearing. Then, without needing to search him, he reached directly into Richard's jacket and plucked the vial from his pocket.

Judas held the vial up to the light, studying both of the fragments they'd recovered. He was pleased with what he saw. He started to smile his thin smile but, before it could widen, he was racked by a convulsion that bent him over, hands on his knees, coughing up something black and vile onto the floor.

"Oh dear," he apologized, wiping the corners of his mouth. "So sorry. You can tell how much I need the gifts that you've brought."

He removed the glove from his right hand and showed it to Cass.

"In fact, you can see the problem for yourself."

He held his hand just inches from her face. The flesh of his hand had deteriorated dramatically. Unlike the creeping black that had only recently clouded his face, his hand was in an advanced state of decomposition. He flexed it for her—the bones of his knuckles clearly exposed through the cracked and flaking skin—but, somehow, his hand was still alive.

"Too many years," he explained, walking away with the vial toward the work benches and equipment on the far side of the room. "I've been confined to the darkness for too many years. I think there may be something about flesh that *needs* the light, that *yearns* to be touched by the sun. And without that light—well, eventually, the flesh turns on itself."

He paused for a moment and looked upward, trying to recall something.

"What was it my old, old friend said so long ago before he condemned me to this interminable darkness? 'The spirit is willing but the flesh is weak.'"

He pulled the cover off a high-powered microscope.

"It took me a long time to diagnose the nature of my problem. And even longer to formulate a solution. The solution snapped into focus for me when I stumbled across a scrap of Mesopotamian myth about shadow demons. The legends said that these shadow demons would feed on the blood of holy men and then, flush with that sacred blood, they could walk freely in the light of the sun."

He laughed.

"Shadows! Walking loose in the light!"

He observed Cass's shadow, cast against the wall by the fire at the other end of the room.

"Imagine snipping it loose," he said, pantomiming a snip with a pair of scissors, "and setting it free. This, Ms. Jones, is the gift you've given me. The power to remain a thing of darkness while no longer being banished from the light."

He adjusted several elements of the microscope.

"With this curse, I've been given a kind of perverse power. I have the power to reproduce what I am with a bite and, thereby, turn others into vampires. I make others like me. But this power has been sharply limited up until now. It's been confined to the darkness all these years."

He switched on a desk lamp.

"But now, unafraid of the light, what will stop me? What will stop me from spreading like a virus without a natural enemy? The world—slowly at first, but then with a kind of exponential inevitability—will be transformed into a reflection of my own image. Jesus Christ himself cursed me with this curse when I betrayed him. But now—now, I'm going to turn that curse into a gift and give birth to an entirely new world. Everyone who survives will become, like me, a shadow. Everyone who survives their old lives will become undead."

Jesus? Cass thought. *Is this guy supposed to be Judas Iscariot himself? One of Jesus' own twelve apostles, the one who betrayed him for thirty pieces of silver?*

Judas watched Cass's face as she put the pieces together. He was pleased.

Cass looked at Richard. "Judas," she said, "as in … Judas Iscariot."

Richard nodded in confirmation.

"That is an old, old name," the thin man said. "Much maligned. But it will do."

Jesus Christ!

Then he turned back to the bench and removed the fragments from the vial.

He continued. "The key, of course, is the *blood*. The cross itself is helpful, but it's not the main event. The cross is a holy relic and, as a relic, it is invested with power by the countless people who *believe* that it has power."

With a pair of tweezers, he placed one of the fragments under the lens of a microscope.

"Billions of minds, past and present, can reshape reality itself with the power of their beliefs, tapping into forces they don't understand with the strength of their convictions, unconsciously wielding magic. Christianity is a case study in exactly this phenomenon: mass delusion bending reality into a corresponding shape. The fact that it is a delusion—that Jesus is no more God than I am—doesn't rob those beliefs of their power."

He was bent over the microscope, fine-tuning the focus. He went silent for a moment, then stood up straight and adjusted his tie. He was obviously disappointed with what he'd seen.

He replaced the first fragment with the second.

"But as I was saying, the blood is the key. And, in my case, *his* blood, Jesus' blood, is the key. That is why I need the One True Cross. As holy relics, the fragments gather and focus the power of that mass delusion we call Christianity. But as fragments of the bloody instrument of torture that robbed Jesus of his life, some of these relics still bear his blood. And that blood will set me free."

Cass noted that the items scattered on his work bench included the weapons that she and Richard had brought with them. In particular, the items included her mother's blade. Her fingers itched just thinking about it.

Judas lapsed into silence, examining the second fragment.

"This," he said, his posture gone rigid, "is *not* the anointed piece."

He spun on his heels and paced sharply in Cass's direction. He stopped immediately in front of Cass and slapped her hard across the face with an open, gloved hand.

"I know that, asshole," Cass said, and spat blood onto his immaculate white shirt.

"Where—where—" Judas stuttered, "where is it!"

He gripped Cass's head between his hands and began to squeeze.

"We are short on time. You will tell me," he coughed, his face just inches from her own, his fetid breath hot on her cheek, "where it is."

"Go to hell," Cass said, slamming her forehead with vicious force into his nose.

Judas stumbled backward, his blackened nose crushed and crumbling.

Cass was seeing stars and had to fight to keep from blacking out herself.

Judas bent over, coughing uncontrollably.

Cass rattled her cuffs again, hard enough that the steel cut deeper into her flesh. She could feel blood dripping from her wrist and off the end of her fingers.

But it was still no use.

Judas recovered, slowed his breathing, and stood upright. He reached up to probe with his finger the ruin of flesh and cartilage that used to be his nose.

"Damn," he said. And then he peeled the black and mangled tissue off his face, exposing the sinus cavity beneath. He tossed the tissue aside. A thin, black fluid trickled out of the cavity.

He straightened his tie and collected himself.

He looked, now, like an impeccably dressed skeleton.

"I apologize for the interruption," he said, his voice wet and nasal. "Now, where were we?"

Cass felt a plunging feeling of despair. She bowed her head and closed her eyes, resting her chin against her breastbone. She felt another wave of anger flickering deep in her chest, but it didn't catch fire.

Then she felt the rough tongue of a cat licking blood from the tip of her finger.

37

"LET'S TRY A different tack," Judas said, returning to his workbench.

He collected the two additional fragments that Cass had brought and carefully inserted them into a kind of golden crown.

He held it up for Cass to see.

"Do you recognize it?" he asked.

The crown consisted of a twisted circlet of thorns, overlaid with ribbons of gold and bound at three points by gold and sky-blue bands.

"The relic of the crown of thorns," Cass realized, "given to Louis IX, King of France, in 1238. It's displayed on the first Friday of every month in the Cathedral of Notre Dame."

"That is correct," Judas confirmed, "except for one detail. It *was* displayed on the first Friday of every month at Notre Dame. Now, obviously, it's here."

He walked back toward her, still carrying the crown.

"Now, as you and I know, this relic is almost certainly fake. But, as I've just explained, we also know that its authenticity isn't decisive. This object has been invested with power either way. And in this case, it strikes me as an especially suitable object for linking and focusing the power of all twenty-nine surviving fragments of the One True Cross that I have painstakingly acquired."

As he neared, Cass could feel a hum of power emanating from the crown. And, too, she could see more clearly how profoundly she had ruined his blackened face.

No collection of holy relics is going to fix that, she thought, swallowing back the bile that was creeping up her throat.

The closer he got, the stronger the hum of power became, until finally the hum coalesced into a throbbing pulse. Cass could felt it thrum through her. And she could feel it most strongly in her weak eye. Her eye throbbed sympathetically with the crown and a spark of heat deep in that socket started to grow. Cass closed her eyes, fighting to gather her attention.

"Ms. Jones," Judas said, snapping his fingers. "Over here."

Cass's eyes fluttered open.

"You look just like her," he said. "It's really quite remarkable. Her face practically shines through yours."

What the hell was he talking about?

Judas registered the look of panic and confusion on her face. Her concentration was shattered.

"Your mother, Ms. Jones. You look just like your mother."

A white hot tongue of anger sprang to life inside of her. Her teeth clenched and her eyes narrowed.

What does this asshole know about my mother?

"Do you know the truth about your mother?" Judas asked. "What lies have they told you? How deep in the dark are you about what happened to her?"

Bastard! Cass screamed in her mind.

Her mother's necklace burned against her breast, as if talking about her had set it on fire. She wasn't sure what that meant, but now that it was lit, the pendant, too, began to throb in sync with the approaching crown.

"Perhaps someday you'll learn what really happened." Judas said. "It's really not for me to say. But what *is* pertinent is the fact that you lost your mother. You are familiar with what it feels like to lose someone you love. You are acquainted with the abyss of pain and grief it leaves inside of you."

Judas paused and positioned the crown on his head. It flared with a pulsing white light. Cass couldn't tell if that light was visible to everyone in the room or just to her, but it was blinding.

"Now, unless you're able to give me the anointed piece, you will lose someone again."

He paused, looking first at Zach and Miranda, still unconscious on the stone floor. But his gaze settled on Richard. He saw the look of panic on her face.

"It didn't take long, did it?" he smiled. "You really shouldn't mix work and love, Ms. Jones. It never works out. Say goodbye to Mr. York."

Judas held out his hands, gathered the throbbing white light emanating from the crown, and shaped it into a crackling ball of energy. Then, like he was some kind of Sith Lord, a stream of white hot electric light shot from his fingers, knocking Richard back onto the floor and breaking his chair. The lightning convulsed his body and Cass swore she could see the occasional, flashing outline of his skeleton through the crackling sparks.

"Nooo!" Cass screamed. Her eye cleared and focused. She could feel the power growing inside of her, time beginning to slow. And she could feel the pendant trembling against her chest, as if it had a life of its own.

"Stop!" she yelled.

Judas paused and gathered the lightning back between his hands.

"This is simple, Ms. Jones. Just tell me where it is."

"I don't know," she yelled over the chaos. "I don't know where it is."

She said it forcefully, aiming to convince Judas of the finality of her answer. But as soon as she'd said it, she doubted the truthfulness of her own statement. She felt her connection to her power—a power dependent on her truthfulness—flicker and dim.

How could I be lying? she wondered. *Why is my power failing? I didn't find the anointed piece! I don't know where it is!*

But even in her own mind, her protest rang hollow.

She could tell that Judas had noted the indecision clouding her face. He had hit a soft spot. There was something there. And he would undoubtedly push harder.

Again he unleashed the lightning and Richard writhed and convulsed on the stone floor.

"He won't be able to take much more of this, Ms. Jones," Judas pressed.

Cass's pendant burned and trembled.

"Do you love him?" he taunted.

Cass didn't dare venture a response to that one.

But Judas didn't stop there.

"Do you believe that God is going to save you? That he will send his angels to defend you? No one is coming to rescue you, Ms. Jones. God is a lie. Jesus can't save you anymore than he could save himself, nailed to that cross, bleeding and powerless."

A surge of power flowed through Judas and into Richard's smoking body and, in response, Cass's pendant flew straight out, as if it were pulled by a powerful magnet, straining against the chain that bound it to Cass.

"DO YOU BELIEVE?" Judas thundered.

Cass searched her own heart, hoping to find some shred of faith in God or Christ or miracles, something she could cling to and put her faith in.

But there was none.

The only bright image she found in her heart was an image of her mother—and of that frozen moment when she had miraculously seen herself through her mother's eyes.

"No," Cass admitted, "I don't believe. I never have."

As she said it, she knew that, this time, she was telling the truth.

She was faithless.

But, too, she was truthful.

And, galvanized by the truth, her body was flooded with a power and light that was not her own, that came from someplace else altogether.

She strained against her handcuffs and stood.

Her chair splintered and the links binding her cuffs snapped.

Her vision expanded and she took in every detail of the room.

She was a Seer.

"Judas!" she roared, shaking off her chains.

38

A CONCUSSIVE WAVE of energy rippled out into the room. Cass was its epicenter. Books, equipment, and henchmen scattered.

Pushed backward, Judas stumbled as an orange tabby darted between his legs.

At the same moment, though, her mother's pendant broke free of its chain and flew across the room, pulled by the cumulative, magnetic power of the other relics Judas had collected.

Judas found his footing and snatched it out of the air.

In the palm of his burning hand, the pendant's casing evaporated.

"Yesss," Judas hissed through his ruined sinus cavity.

Oh shit, Cass thought.

Some buried part of Cass had known all along. She'd worn that pendant around her neck every day for fifteen years and, since the day her mother had given it to her, she'd been following its silent call. She'd been drawn into years of research, into graduate work and a dissertation, and into this final mad scramble for the other fragments of the One True Cross by the gift her mother had left her: the anointed piece.

Her whole life had been spent trying to find something she already had.

But now she'd lost it.

And now Judas held the final piece of the puzzle in the palm of his hand.

Figures, Cass concluded. *You can't make this stuff up.*

Richard lay in a smoking heap next to her, groaning, his clothes in tatters, the wicked scars across his back visible.

What haven't you been telling me? How did you already know Judas? What's your endgame?

She slung one of his arms around her neck and dragged him out of immediate danger, leaving him next to Zach and Miranda in the corner of the room.

Judas, meanwhile, had inserted the final, bloody piece of the cross into his crown of thorns.

He was lifted off the ground by the attendant power. He floated a foot above the ground with his hands outstretched.

And then, for just a moment, crouching next to her friends, Cass thought that it was over. That it was too late. That she'd lost and that he'd won.

In that moment, Cass saw Judas as if he were lit up from within, his muscles and organs became translucent and the bones of this skeleton glowed white. She could see all of his black and rotting flesh healed and his nose repaired and the marks left by time's slow passage erased.

He was clean.

He was beautiful.

Cass felt like she was seeing what God would see were he to smile down on Judas. Or, she felt like she was seeing what Jesus must have seen in Judas when he'd trusted him with his life.

Cass felt a rush of melancholy compassion for this cursed man.

Judas spun gently in the air, turning toward Cass, a look of triumph and satisfaction on his healed and self-possessed face. A storm of roiling light swirled around him.

"Goodbye, Ms. Jones," he said.

39

BUT THE SMILE on Judas's face didn't last long.

The storm of roiling light started to fill with dark clouds and the thorns in Judas's crown began to dig deep into the flesh of his scalp. With a look of horror, Judas began to writhe and tug at the crown. His limbs bent in unnatural directions and his body began to collapse inward, as if he were a sheet of paper being crumpled and thrown away.

The crown, though, was not coming off.

Judas's face was wracked with pain and his body twisted in the air, wrestling with the crown.

The anointed piece, displayed as the centerpiece of the crown, slid downward and pierced his forehead, sinking through skin and bone and into his brain.

Judas's eyes widened and his body now hung in the air, limp and still. The clouds swirling around him slowed and flickered from black to white.

He stared straight ahead, pale and inquisitive.

A revelation dawned across his face.

Then he spoke.

"My God," he whispered. "Dear God … it's true."

Tears streamed down his face.

Cass was riveted, frozen in place until, out of the corner of her eye, she caught sight of Atlantis darting across the room and onto a workbench. The cat deftly wove its way through an array of equipment until, at the end of the bench, it stopped and looked directly at Cass.

My sword.

Cass leapt into action, taking advantage of the lull.

She saw Richard stagger back to his feet, but couldn't worry about that now.

She hurdled a box of equipment and summersaulted into a crouch in front of the workbench.

Atlantis purred.

The walls of the castle were beginning to shake and tremble. Cass didn't like the look of it. She needed to act fast.

She snatched her sword off the bench.

The storm surrounding Judas had gone black again and the winds were picking up speed.

From the center of the vortex Judas cried out in agony, "Father in Heaven, I believe! Have mercy on me!"

Chunks of rock began falling from the ceiling.

Richard had lurched into the center of the room.

Cass doubted that any gods were going to help Judas now. But that didn't mean she couldn't offer him mercy.

With a running start, she launched herself into the air and swung her sword through a mighty arc that passed cleanly through Judas's neck, neatly separating his head from his body.

He was free.

His head and body turned to ash.

The ash was immediately sucked into the vortex.

The crown of thorns clattered to the ground at Richard's feet.

The loose anointed fragment of the cross spun for an instant in the wind until Cass reached out and plucked it from the air.

The castle was disintegrating around them.

Cass and Richard locked eyes through the storm and, maybe for the first time, she saw him simply, plainly as he was. There was no pretense left. She could see that this was the real Richard. This was the truth.

But, as always, she couldn't tell what that truth meant. She couldn't feel, in the first person, the force of it.

As she thought this, a huge section of the stone ceiling came crashing down between them, separating her from Richard.

When the dust cleared, Cass could only see a ton of crushed stone piled where Richard had stood.

"Richard!" she screamed, her throat raw, the anointed piece biting into the palm of her clenched fist.

Stones continued to fall and she felt Atlantis brush against her leg, his tail curling and pulling her toward Zach and Miranda. Both were awake and struggling to get their legs under them. Supporting them both, Cass led them out of the room and down the hall toward the entrance.

They burst through the main door and into the open air, cutting through a billowing fog of dust and debris and ran for the edge of the forest.

They sheltered at the foot of an ancient tree, a safe distance from the castle, and watched the remainder of the castle collapse with thunderous rumble.

Atlantis wasn't with them, but Cass wasn't worried.

Richard, on the other hand—she didn't see how *anyone* could have survived that.

Whatever strength Cass had left vanished. She fell to her knees and leaned into Zach, who pulled her close.

The dust began to settle and the sun, just creeping above the rim of the mountain, shone through the morning fog, burning it away.

Epilogue

THE VIDEO WAS grainy and lacked color, but it was good enough. It was obviously shot from long distance through a telephoto lens. There was no audio.

The video showed Cass, at home in Salem, with Zach and a machinist.

Cass was smiling and joking playfully with Zach. Her tight white t-shirt flattered her slim, athletic figure. The sun shone in her black hair.

The machinist was working to incorporate an ancient fragment of wood into the hilt of her mother's sword. The result would be a kind of "anointed blade."

When he'd finished, the machinist handed the blade to Cass and, as she hefted it, her smile disappeared. She was all business now. She swung the sword through a series of strokes, leaving an almost visible trail of light in the wake of each stroke.

She was obviously pleased with the sword. But she also looked sad. When she had the sword in her hand, she looked like she was carrying a weight that, alone, she wasn't sure she could bear.

Richard rewound the video and watched it again.

The hospital-grade monitoring equipment in his private room beeped weakly and irregularly in time with his unsteady heart.

The battered crown of thorns lay on his bedside table.

He was covered from head to toe in a variety of plaster casts. His nose was broken, his eyes black and bloodshot. He could barely move anything but the finger that rested on the video controls.

They'd succeeded in gathering up most of the fragments of the One True Cross, but things hadn't gone quite to plan. Things had gotten complicated. Cassandra had gotten complicated. Now he would have to decide how to proceed. And what price he was willing to pay.

But—like it or not—he had time to think about it.

Soon enough, their real work could begin.

He rewound the video again and started it from the beginning.

He watched the blade dance in her hand, the sun in her hair.

She was beautiful.

Thank you for reading *Faithless*, book 1 of A Vision of Vampires. If you enjoyed the book, please consider leaving a review on Amazon.com—your support is very much appreciated!

Sign up to find out about new books from Laura Legend, including new books in A Vision of Vampires:

www.smarturl.it/legendaries

Other Books by Laura Legend

Hopeless: A Vision of Vampires 2

Blameless: A Vision of Vampires 3

Fearless: A Vision of Vampires 4

Timeless: A Vision of Vampires 5

Contact information:

www.lauralegendwrites.com

facebook.com/lauralegendwrites/

laura@lauralegendwrites.com

573-405-1607